Acting Edition

The Timing of a Day

by Owen Panettieri

Copyright © 2025 by Owen Panettieri
All Rights Reserved

THE TIMING OF A DAY is fully protected under the copyright laws of the United States of America, the British Commonwealth, including Canada, and all member countries of the Berne Convention for the Protection of Literary and Artistic Works, the Universal Copyright Convention, and/or the World Trade Organization conforming to the Agreement on Trade Related Aspects of Intellectual Property Rights. All rights, including professional and amateur stage productions, recitation, lecturing, public reading, motion picture, radio broadcasting, television, online/digital production, and the rights of translation into foreign languages are strictly reserved.

ISBN 978-0-573-71201-2

www.concordtheatricals.com
www.concordtheatricals.co.uk

FOR PRODUCTION INQUIRIES

UNITED STATES AND CANADA
info@concordtheatricals.com
1-866-979-0447

UNITED KINGDOM AND EUROPE
licensing@concordtheatricals.co.uk
020-7054-7298

Each title is subject to availability from Concord Theatricals Corp., depending upon country of performance. Please be aware that *THE THE TIMING OF A DAY* may not be licensed by Concord Theatricals Corp. in your territory. Professional and amateur producers should contact the nearest Concord Theatricals Corp. office or licensing partner to verify availability.

CAUTION: Professional and amateur producers are hereby warned that *THE TIMING OF A DAY* is subject to a licensing fee. The purchase, renting, lending or use of this book does not constitute a license to perform this title(s), which license must be obtained from Concord Theatricals Corp. prior to any performance. Performance of this title(s) without a license is a violation of federal law and may subject the producer and/or presenter of such performances to civil penalties. Both amateurs and professionals considering a production are strongly advised to apply to the appropriate agent before starting rehearsals, advertising, or booking a theatre. A licensing fee must be paid whether the title(s) is presented for charity or gain and whether or not admission is charged. Professional/Stock licensing fees are quoted upon application to Concord Theatricals Corp.

This work is published by Samuel French, an imprint of Concord Theatricals Corp.

No one shall make any changes in this title(s) for the purpose of production. No part of this book may be reproduced, stored in a retrieval system, scanned, uploaded, or transmitted in any form, by any means, now known or yet to be invented, including mechanical, electronic, digital, photocopying, recording, videotaping, or otherwise, without the prior written permission of the publisher. No one shall share this title(s), or any part of this title(s), through any social media or file hosting websites.

For all inquiries regarding motion picture, television, online/digital and other media rights, please contact Concord Theatricals Corp.

MUSIC AND THIRD-PARTY MATERIALS USE NOTE

Licensees are solely responsible for obtaining formal written permission from copyright owners to use copyrighted music and/or other copyrighted third-party materials (e.g. artworks, logos) in the performance of this play and are strongly cautioned to do so. If no such permission is obtained by the licensee, then the licensee must use only original music and materials that the licensee owns and controls. Licensees are solely responsible and liable for clearances of all third-party copyrighted materials, including without limitation music, and shall indemnify the copyright owners of the play(s) and their licensing agent, Concord Theatricals Corp., against any costs, expenses, losses and liabilities arising from the use of such copyrighted third-party materials by licensees. For music, please contact the appropriate music licensing authority in your territory for the rights to any incidental music.

IMPORTANT BILLING AND CREDIT REQUIREMENTS

If you have obtained performance rights to this title, please refer to your licensing agreement for important billing and credit requirements.

THE TIMING OF A DAY was first produced as part of the New York International Fringe Festival by Mind The Art Entertainment in association with Intimation Theater, premiering on August 18, 2010. The production was directed by Joey Brenneman, and the production stage manager was Paul Jason Baker. The cast was as follows:

DOUG . . . . Niko Kourtis
PAIGE. . . . . .R. Elizabeth Woodard
JOSH . . . . .Adam Shorsten
MATTY. . . . . Justin Anselmi

THE TIMING OF A DAY was subsequently produced at Center Stage in New York City by Mind The Art Entertainment in association with Intimation Theater, opening on March 30, 2011. The production was directed by Joey Brenneman, with scenic design by Jared Rutherford, lighting design by Maricel Greene, and sound design by Michael Berberich. The executive producer was Christian De Gré Cárdenas, along with producer Ariana Paganetti, co-producers Jesse R. Tendler and Owen Panettieri, and associate producer Winter Williams. The technical director was Joseph Reese Anderson. The publicist was Les Schecter and the box office manager was Cheryl Moy. The assistant director was David Williams, the production stage manager was Daniella Caggiano, and the assistant stage manager was Grace Sumner. The cast was as follows:

DOUG . . . . Niko Kourtis
PAIGE. . . . . .R. Elizabeth Woodard
JOSH . . . . Migs Govea
MATTY. . . . . Justin Anselmi

CHARACTERS

DOUG – roommate; a dancer, gay, late 20s, male

PAIGE – roommate; an actress/activist, mid-20s, female

JOSH – roommate; an office admin, late 20s, male

MATTY – Paige's off-and-on boyfriend, early 20s, male

SETTING

The play takes place in a three-bedroom apartment
in Harlem, New York.

TIME

The day is comprised of:

1. Ordinary Morning, January 13, 2009 – 8:30 a.m.
2. Forever Afternoon, January 27, 2009 – 12:30 p.m.
3. Dinner with Friends, March 6, 2007 – 5:30 p.m.
4. The Loneliness of Evening, July 10, 2007 – 8:30 p.m.
5. Stumbling Through the Dark, July 8, 2008 – 11:45 p.m.
6. Living After Midnight, November 5, 2008 – 2:00 a.m.
7. Watch the Sunrise, January 28, 2009 – 4:30 a.m.
8. I Hope Tomorrow Is Like Today, Somewhen

NOTE ON DIALOGUE

/ indicates the next line should start before the current line is completed.

PLAYWRIGHT'S NOTE

This is a story about timing and expectations. Some things we think we'll never see in our lifetimes actually come to pass, and some things that we think will naturally come to us just never materialize. This is also a story about love shared in small moments and words that carry weight over time, even if we hardly remember them.

These characters have a complicated history that refuses to let itself be told linearly. Even though events are presented out of order, the cycle of the day marches on from one sunrise to the next, because no matter how often we go back to replay certain moments in our minds, time is always moving forward. In terms of the dialogue, the delivery is intended to be quick and crisp, with conversations continually flowing forward. They are New Yorkers. We walk fast and we talk fast in this city.

The transitions between the scenes can be a great opportunity to build out the world of the roommates. I love what original director Joey Brenneman crafted for the premiere runs of the show and encourage future directors to explore how they can utilize the transitions in a meaningful way.

So many wonderful people helped me throughout the writing process of this play. I am especially grateful to my earliest readers: Amanda Kay Crystal, Sarah Levithan Daniels, Una LaMarche, and Lin-Manuel Miranda. Jennifer Lauren Brown and David Dean Carl also provided great insight and support during the revision process. Thank you to Nancy A. Rose, Esq., Charmaine Ferenczi, and Victoria Wong for their counsel and support throughout this play's publication process.

Thank you to the tremendous cast and crew of both the FringeNYC and Center Stage, NY, runs of *The Timing of a Day*. The team at Mind The Art Entertainment worked tirelessly and with great enthusiasm in producing the initial run of the show. I'm so glad we took this journey together.

Finally, thank you to my husband, Josh Blye (who only coincidentally shares a name with a character in this play), for being my constant support and for always sharing his time and his love with me every day.

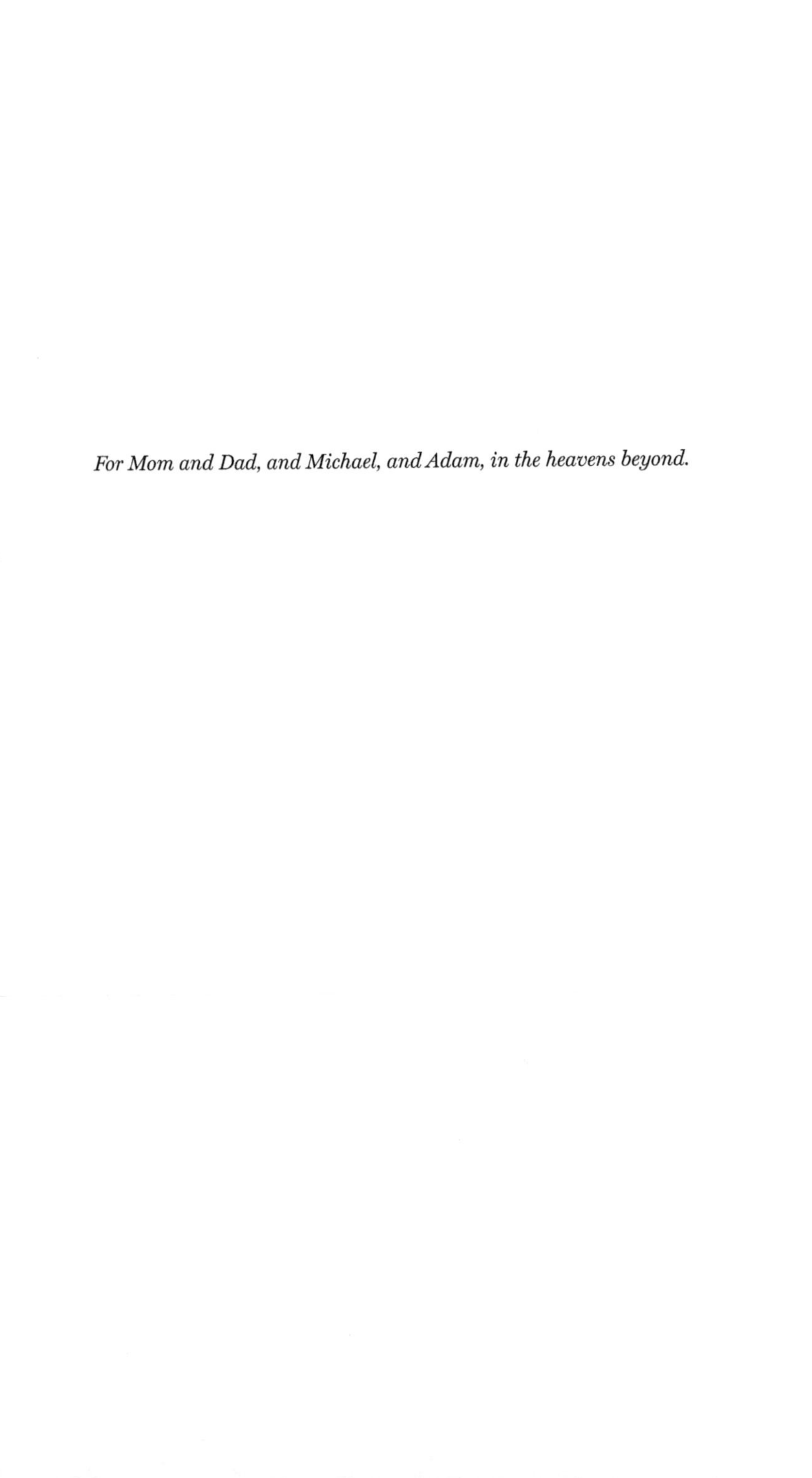

For Mom and Dad, and Michael, and Adam, in the heavens beyond.

1. Ordinary Morning

(January 13, 2009 – 8:30 a.m. An apartment in Harlem, New York.)

(The morning sun spills in from the kitchen window. The only other light comes from the TV that's on in the living room. The furniture has all been picked up by the tenants at different times from different places, and it's all seen better days. Behind the living room couch, we see a small sunken-in hallway, with the bathroom door facing out to the audience. To the left and the right of the bathroom are unseen doors leading to two bedrooms. Moving from stage right to left, the living room bleeds into the kitchen area, with the big appliances on the upstage wall. The door on the upstage right wall leads to a third bedroom, and downstage left is the door leading out of the apartment.)

*(The apartment is a cluttered mess, but for all its faults, the space is welcoming and has a spirit of fun about it. Framed pictures, posters, and art hang on the walls. The nicest thing in the apartment is the kitchen table and chairs, which are a complete set. The table [which splits center stage with the living room couch] is cluttered with mail and cereal boxes and perhaps a stray Christmas decoration that never got put away. **DOUG**, a dancer in his late twenties, is sitting on the couch watching the TV with the sound muted. He is wearing*

large headphones and is bopping his head to music we don't hear. He stares at the screen. His face is tense. He is thinking. **PAIGE**, *a woman in her mid-twenties, enters from the upstage right bedroom, looking like hell. She is sick with God-knows-what, but insists on willing herself through her morning routine as if she is fine. She looks out the window and groans.* **DOUG** *notices her and takes off his headphones.*)

DOUG. Good morning!

PAIGE. *(Sing-song.)* No, it's not. 'Cause I'm awake!

DOUG. Sleep okay?

PAIGE. Not really. I feel like I had crazy dreams, but I can't remember them now. You know when you have that?

DOUG. Uh huh. It's the worst.

PAIGE. Josh up yet?

DOUG. Just got out of the shower. Bathroom's all yours.

PAIGE. I can't believe how late I slept. I'm supposed to be leaving now. I just can't wake up…

DOUG. There's coffee if you want coffee.

PAIGE. I wish. My throat's still killing me.

DOUG. Still?

PAIGE. STILL. It's really bad this morning.

DOUG. Test results come back…?

PAIGE. Tomorrow, supposedly.

DOUG. Paige, I really think it's mono.

PAIGE. Ugh, it can't be mono. That shit will never go away.

DOUG. Sorry, babe. You've had this thing too long.

PAIGE. Dougie, you're supposed to tell me it's not serious and it's gonna go away.

DOUG. *(With no conviction.)* It's not serious and it's gonna go away.

PAIGE. Thanks.

(She goes to look out the window.)

Is it supposed to effing snow today?

DOUG. NY1 just said partly cloudy. No snow.

PAIGE. They are such LIARS. Look out a FUCKING WINDOW NY1!

DOUG. It's gonna be cold. Dress warm.

PAIGE. This sucks.

(She scratches at her throat.)

How are *you*, Dougie?

*(**PAIGE** goes through the kitchen cabinets looking for a bottle of apple cider vinegar. She does not hear what **DOUG** is about to tell her.)*

DOUG. I'm alright. My head really hurts.

PAIGE. Uh huh...

DOUG. I fell on the stairs coming down Morningside Park last night. There was ice, and I didn't see it, and I totally wiped out a couple steps before the landing. I got lucky though. Just a little banged up.

*(**DOUG** notices she isn't listening.)*

And then on my way out of the park, I met this guy who had pandas with him and we had sex with the pandas.

*(**PAIGE** finds the apple cider vinegar.)*

PAIGE. Found it! ...Wait, what with the pandas? What the fuck are you talking about?

DOUG. You weren't listening. I started making shit up.

PAIGE. Sorry, what were you saying?

DOUG. Doesn't matter. It's fine –

PAIGE. No, I'm sorry. I just got distracted with this. Hold on.

(*She swigs the vinegar, gargles loudly.*)

DOUG. What the hell are you doing?

(*She spits into the sink.*)

PAIGE. I'm gargling. I'm *trying* to gargle, but this shit tastes *so bad*.

DOUG. What is it?

PAIGE. Apple cider vinegar. Amber told me at work that when you have a sore throat, if you gargle with organic apple cider vinegar, it clears it up right away. I figured I'd try it.

(*She aggressively rubs her throat.*)

I just wanna dig in and rip the whole thing out at this point.

DOUG. Call in sick so you can rest.

PAIGE. I called in sick last week. First Thought doesn't give paid sick days. If you'd like me to have my share of the rent this month, then I'm gonna have to go to work at some point.

DOUG. C'mon, Josh will cover you if you're short.

(*She gives him a look.*)

Since you're sick! He spotted me last month. He'll do it for you.

(**JOSH**, *a friendly-faced dude in his late twenties, enters from his bedroom, stage left of the bathroom, dressed in business clothes for work.*)

JOSH. What will he do for you?

PAIGE. Look good in a fitted dress shirt. That's what he'll do. Oww!

(*She grabs her throat from sharp pain.*)

Oww...

JOSH. How you feeling?

PAIGE. Like shit. How 'bout you?

JOSH. Hmm...better than that, thankfully.

DOUG. She finds out if it's mono tomorrow.

PAIGE. (*Convincing herself.*) It's not.

JOSH. I kinda want it to turn out to be esophageal gonorrhea.

DOUG. Eww! What's that?

JOSH. Is it in the lesson plan for today?

PAIGE. Today is contraception.

DOUG. Hello? What's the gono-thingy?

(**JOSH** *gets close to* **DOUG**'*s face.*)

JOSH. (*Making it sound sexy/dirty.*) Esophageal gonorrhea is gonorrhea in your throat.

DOUG. You can get that there?

JOSH. In fact, you can. You should really be more aware of shit like this. You're high risk.

DOUG. I am not! Not lately anyway. So I'm not getting your esophogoalie – whatever you called it.

JOSH. – Esophageal gonorrhea. –

DOUG. Yeah, that. No thanks.

PAIGE. Well, I'd fucking take it. I know how that's treated, and then it would GO AWAY.

JOSH. In the meantime, there's your new Facebook status. "Paige is throat gono!"

PAIGE. It is NOT throat gono. You're such a dork.

*(She playfully hits **JOSH**. He likes it.)*

But if it *was,* I'd know exactly who I got it from and would proceed to totally kick his ass.

DOUG. I didn't think you and Matty were exclusive anymore.

*(**JOSH** makes a face at mention of **MATTY**.)*

PAIGE. We're not, but he's the only guy I do *that* with *that* way, so –

DOUG. Ahh, gotcha.

JOSH. Have you guys seen my Blackberry lying around?

DOUG. No. This is why I got you that dish for Christmas, so you could put it there and not lose it. Why are you not using the Berry Bowl?

JOSH. I know, I know.

DOUG. I decorated it and everything!

JOSH. I love the Berry Bowl. The Berry Bowl is awesome. I just always put it down weird places without realizing. Is it in the couch?

*(He reaches into the couch cushions around **DOUG** playfully.)*

DOUG. Get off!

(**DOUG** *dumps* **JOSH** *off onto the floor. He takes this opportunity to look under the couch and coffee table. No dice.*)

It's not here.

JOSH. Fuuuuck. I don't have time to go on a big search for it.

(**JOSH** *exits to his room to search.*)

PAIGE. Doofus.

(*To* **DOUG**.) Why are you watching that with no sound?

DOUG. Cuz they've cycled through all the news once and I don't want to hear it again.

PAIGE. So just turn it off.

DOUG. No. I wanna look at Pat Kiernan some more.

PAIGE. You and Pat Kiernan.

DOUG. He's cute!

PAIGE. What time are you going into work?

(*She goes back into the kitchen.*)

DOUG. Noon.

PAIGE. Then why the hell are you up?

DOUG. Can't sleep. I have a headache. I'm waiting to take some more Motrin in like an hour.

PAIGE. Just go to sleep.

(*She looks at the clock.*)

I should be out the door already.

DOUG. The hospital's like three minutes away.

PAIGE. I'm not going to the hospital. I have to teach a workshop in the Bronx in like forty-five minutes. Have you seen my binder?

DOUG. Check the table. High school or middle school?

PAIGE. Today is high school. The class isn't bad… It just sucks getting there by the subway.

> (**JOSH** *reenters with laptop and charger. He puts the laptop on the table for* **PAIGE** *and rather absently carries the charger in his hand.*)

JOSH. So just take a cab today.

PAIGE. I already bought my Metrocard and that takes care of my transportation budget for January.

> (*She spots the binder on the chair.*)

Found it!

JOSH. My Blackberry?

PAIGE. No, my binder.

JOSH. Grr… Doug, can you –

DOUG. On it.

> (*He picks up his phone before* **JOSH** *can ask, and calls Josh's cell. There is a buzzing sound in the kitchen.* **PAIGE** *uses the laptop.*)

PAIGE. The kitchen is vibrating.

> (**JOSH** *opens a drawer and pulls out the Blackberry.*)

JOSH. Yes! Got it.

DOUG. Where?

JOSH. Utensil drawer.

DOUG. *Utensil* drawer?

> (**JOSH** *notices the bottle of vinegar.*)

JOSH. What's this?

PAIGE. Amber told me to gargle with that for my throat.

JOSH. Don't take that shit. It won't work.

PAIGE. Amber swears by it.

JOSH. Well, Amber doesn't know shit!

PAIGE. Well, I need to try *something*.

JOSH. I'm gonna be late.

(He exits to his room.)

DOUG. Any good e-mails?

PAIGE. Hmm? No… I was hoping to get a message about a callback, but there's nothing.

DOUG. Sorry.

PAIGE. Whatever, no big loss.

*(**JOSH** rushes back in and points to the laptop.)*

JOSH. Okay, I'm gonna need that back. I can't be late today.

DOUG. Scarf?

JOSH. Scarf…

*(He spins back around and exits into his room again. **DOUG** and **PAIGE** share a snarky look.)*

DOUG. I want cereal.

*(He moves toward the kitchen to gather supplies, **PAIGE** rifles through her binder at the table.)*

Are you gonna take a shower? That'll make you feel a little better.

PAIGE. I don't have the time or energy to shower. They can smell me today.

DOUG. What's your plan post-work?

PAIGE. Let's see: I'm teaching this morning, meeting Matty for a late lunch, picking up dry cleaning, and then coming home to sleep FOREVER.

DOUG. If you do too much, it makes it worse.

PAIGE. I know. Thank you, Doctor Doug.

DOUG. And take Tylenol every four hours to keep your fever down.

PAIGE. I will, Doctor.

DOUG. I had mono, jerk. I'm trying to help you.

PAIGE. I know. I appreciate it.

(**JOSH** *re-enters.*)

JOSH. Okay, scarf. Blackberry. iPod. Laptop. I am good to go.

PAIGE. Keys?

JOSH. Keys!

DOUG. Bathroom. Soap dish.

JOSH. Really?

(He goes to look in the bathroom.)

DOUG. Yes, I know I saw those there this morning.

JOSH. Yes! Awesome.

DOUG. *(Trills.)* Yeaaah!

JOSH. *(He mimics* **DOUG**.*)* Yeaaah! Thanks!

DOUG. You're welcome. Sit down and eat something.

JOSH. No time! I'll grab something on the way.

DOUG. Suuuure. Manorexic.

JOSH. I will! Okay, computer in the bag and I'm out of here.

DOUG. We're hanging out tonight?

JOSH. I think so. I'll call you later. You're gonna –

DOUG. Be downtown. And don't forget we have to work –

JOSH. On your birthday e-vite. We will, old man, we will.

PAIGE. My two princes turning thirty! Craaaazy!

JOSH. Hey, I've still got over a month, don't rush me! Okay, feel better.

(*To* **DOUG**.) I'll call you later.

PAIGE. Bye.

JOSH. Bye!

> (**JOSH** *exits. They sit in silence for a moment as* **DOUG** *eats.* **PAIGE** *notices the laptop charger on the counter.*)

PAIGE. Oh, he forgot the charger again.

DOUG. (*He rubs his temples.*) He'll be back. He'll check it before getting to the train.

PAIGE. Doug? Wanna do me a favor?

DOUG. No. What is it?

PAIGE. You wanna go teach a bunch of really great, *really* attentive high school kids about methods of contraception for me so I can stay here and sleep?

DOUG. Not so much.

PAIGE. Curse you.

DOUG. I am cursed.

> (**PAIGE** *pretends to zap* **DOUG** *with her hands and makes a spell-casting noise then promptly starts hack coughing.*)

DOUG. Just calm down. See what happens when you act evil?

PAIGE. How long is this gonna last, D?

DOUG. If it's mono, it can stay with you for a long time. It was really six months or so before all the symptoms went away for me.

PAIGE. *Six months?*

DOUG. It depends how bad it is.

PAIGE. Matty is gonna break up with me.

DOUG. You guys break up all the time.

PAIGE. Well this time for good. I'm gonna be a bad girlfriend who has no energy to do anything and just wants to complain all the time.

DOUG. You can always complain to me.

PAIGE. You promise?

DOUG. Promise. You can complain to me and fight with Josh and give all your nice time to Matty.

PAIGE. He doesn't deserve all of it.

    (She slumps.)

DOUG. *(He taps his neck.)* Energy!

PAIGE. *(She taps her neck halfheartedly.)* Energy! Okay, coat...

DOUG. Maybe you should put on real pants?

PAIGE. Yeah, that would help. Do you have anything lined up this week?

    (She exits to her room as they talk.)

DOUG. Chorus calls Thursday and Friday. It's a national tour on Friday. It'd be awesome if I got that.

PAIGE. If you're on tour, how am I gonna complain to you? You're already breaking promises!

DOUG. You can call. Text.

(**PAIGE** *re-enters in better casual clothing.*)

PAIGE. Texting. The height of human comfort.

DOUG. Well then hope that it's esophogono–whatnot and that drugs will clean it right up.

(*She sits back down at table and labors over her shoes. She smiles.*)

PAIGE. That's so gross. Josh is gross.

DOUG. He nasty! It's too bad you can't come out with us tonight.

(**PAIGE** *gets up to get her coat. Her gloves are on the table.*)

PAIGE. Boys' night out. If you come home and I'm sprawled out on the floor, please just step over me.

DOUG. We'll roll you out of the way of foot traffic. Don't worry.

PAIGE. Thanks! Okay I'm off.

DOUG. You're my hero, Paige!

PAIGE. Awesome. That will carry me through. I'm not kissing you, cuz I'm sick.

DOUG. Oh-kaaay...

PAIGE. Bye, babe! Talk to you later.

(**DOUG** *sees her gloves on the table.*)

DOUG. (*With a mouth full of cereal.*) Gah yug lovz.

(*She doesn't get what he's saying.*)

PAIGE. Uh, okay. Later!

(She exits. He swallows.)

DOUG. Yeah, you'll be back for those.

> *(**DOUG** keeps eating. He rubs his head, swallows and sits still. There is a low buzzing sound that builds. It's the sound of a light bulb about to burst. The pain in **DOUG**'s head builds. The sound builds. He pushes the bowl away from him and puts his head down on the table. He has the spoon in his hand and is tapping it against the table. The sound builds and then there is a pop.)*
>
> *(The tapping of the spoon stops. **DOUG**'s fingers loosen and the spoon falls. Lights out.)*

Transition

2. Forever Afternoon

(January 27, 2009 – 12:30 p.m.)

(Two weeks later. A grey day. There is considerably less of both **DOUG** *and* **PAIGE** *in the space. The table and chairs are gone. Boxes have replaced some of the clutter. There are some heavy ghosts here now. The buzzer rings.* **JOSH** *enters from his room and hits the buzzer by the front door. He unlocks the door and then moves all the way back into the living room.* **MATTY,** *an easily likable guy in his early twenties, enters, carrying a duffle bag.* **PAIGE** *follows, intensely rummaging through her purse.)*

JOSH. Hey.

MATTY. Hey man, how you doing? Good to see ya.

JOSH. Yeah, you too, Matty.

   (To **PAIGE**.*)* Hey.

PAIGE. Hey.

JOSH. How are ya?

PAIGE. The keys were in my bag when we left. I don't know where the hell they went.

JOSH. It's no big deal.

MATTY. Here, do you want me to –

PAIGE. No, I will find them.

   (She avoids eye contact with both of them, continues to shove stuff around in her bag.)

MATTY. Elevator's back up!

JOSH. Yeah, one of those rare days…

(**PAIGE** *pulls the keys out of her bag.*)

PAIGE. Ahh! Got them! See?

MATTY. Great!

PAIGE. I told you they were in there.

MATTY. I know. I believed you.

(**PAIGE** *turns away, finally bringing herself
to look around.*)

JOSH. Hey, I heard you had quite an adventure at
Inauguration.

MATTY. Yeah. Purple Gate. It sucked. I mean the whole
trip was great, but the Gate was – that was another
story. It was fucking cold too, dude.

JOSH. It looked really cold.

MATTY. *So* fucking cold. I mean we didn't really care, it
was so exciting…but Paige had the right idea to stay
home. She would not have liked the cold.

(*He looks toward* **PAIGE**, *who continues to
stare around the apartment.*)

Y'okay?

PAIGE. How are you staying here?

JOSH. Well, where am I supposed to go?

PAIGE. I know, but…

MATTY. Hey, can I trouble you for some water?

JOSH. Yeah. Help yourself. Brita's in the fridge. There's
other shit there too. Have whatever.

MATTY. Water's good. Paige?

PAIGE. It's not good on my throat!

MATTY. Right! I forgot. Sorry.

(He goes to the fridge.)

PAIGE. My fucking throat still hurts, can you believe that? Seems the only thing that doesn't hurt it right now is cream soda.

JOSH. Cream soda?

*(**MATTY** goes looking for a glass in the cabinets, **PAIGE** and **JOSH** move a little bit away from him.)*

PAIGE. Yeah, Joshy, do you happen to have any cream soda?

JOSH. I am out of cream soda.

PAIGE. Sucks for me.

JOSH. How ya been?

PAIGE. Not good.

JOSH. *(Almost breaking.)* I've *missed* you.

*(**PAIGE** gives him a hard stare then turns to **MATTY**.)*

PAIGE. Hey, babe? Can you go downstairs and get me a cream soda from the bodega? I feel my throat closing up already. I'm really gonna need it.

MATTY. Okay, what like a two-liter?

PAIGE. No, not like a two-liter. Like just a normal-size drink...size.

MATTY. Okay, okay. Be back in a minute.

PAIGE. Take the keys!

(She throws him the keys. He exits.)

He's trying to be supportive.

JOSH. How's that working out for him?

PAIGE. I yell at him and cry a lot and then I don't put out. It's really great. He loves it.

JOSH. He cares about you.

PAIGE. Swell.

JOSH. I've been trying to call you since –

PAIGE. I know. I'm – I haven't called anyone back for like two weeks now, so…

JOSH. I'm "anyone"?

PAIGE. No. I just needed…

JOSH. What?

PAIGE. Space. Some post-funeral space.

JOSH. And now?

PAIGE. Now… I require slightly less space.

JOSH. Paige…

PAIGE. I really can't talk about stuff right now. You told me I had to come, so I'm here. Let's just stick to the bullshitting till we're done. Okay?

JOSH. Okay… You just wanna –

PAIGE. Yup.

JOSH. Okay…

(They head over to the couch.)

His folks came by earlier this week and took a bunch of stuff, but they wanted us to look through the rest of it before they come back again.

PAIGE. They took the table?

JOSH. Um, no. I just kinda left it out on the street. It was gone in fifteen minutes.

PAIGE. You left it out?

JOSH. I didn't know what to do with it. I didn't wanna keep it. I mean, there wasn't really anything wrong with it.

PAIGE. Except our friend died on it.

JOSH. There wasn't any – the stuff they left that we have to look through is in these boxes.

PAIGE. Can I have his Discman?

(**JOSH** *knew this was coming.*)

JOSH. They took the Discman.

PAIGE. Are you fucking kidding me? They took it?

JOSH. They asked for it. I had to give it to them.

PAIGE. Noooooo. I really wanted it!

JOSH. You could ask them for it.

PAIGE. No. I can't ask for it. They want it for the same reason I do. Bulky old-school Discman, with the giant headphones. So cute.

JOSH. Anti-iPod to his very last day.

PAIGE. Tell me they didn't take all his mix CDs?

JOSH. I gave them all the discs but two. I kept "Great Adventures Mix '07" for me and for you "Bathroom Tunes Spring '08."

PAIGE. YES. My favorite! That kid loved the bathroom. Weirdo. Are you keeping any of his clothes?

JOSH. Uhh...some of the shirts.

PAIGE. What about his pajama pants? Did they leave his pajama pants?

JOSH. They did in fact leave the pajama pants.

PAIGE. Can I have them? I want them.

JOSH. Sure... I'm keeping the D.A.R.E. T-shirt.

(She stares after **JOSH** *for a second. Weighs her options. Lets it pass.)*

PAIGE. D.A.R.E., yeah you should. It looks good on you.

JOSH. I can wear an old dryer-shrunken T-shirt, it's true.

*(***PAIGE*** switches boxes around.)*

A lot of it is kinda random. He was a bit of a pack rat.

PAIGE. Yeah, but…this is just stuff. I don't even think it's all his stuff. It's just…

(She pulls out tampons from the box.)

I think these are mine, even. What the fuck? His folks really cleaned up on the good stuff, didn't they?

JOSH. It's all they have left of him.

PAIGE. Hmm.

(She is ready to explode, but pushes it down again. She angrily rummages around in the box. **JOSH** *is at a bit of a loss as to what to do. He gets an idea.)*

JOSH. I finally got those pictures from Election Night developed. You wanna look through?

(He goes to get them off a shelf.)

PAIGE. I hate me in pictures.

*(***JOSH*** goes to put them down.)*

Okay, gimme.

(He hands them to her. She looks them over.)

Fat. Fat.

JOSH. STOP. You are not fat in any of those.

PAIGE. Fat. *Wasted.* Amber looks really good in this one, but of course I'm blinking. This is a wonderful trip down mem–

> *(She stops. There is a picture of* **PAIGE**, **DOUG**, *and* **JOSH** *wrapped up on their couch. This hits* **PAIGE** *hard.)*

I totally forgot about this one.

JOSH. Which one?

> *(She flips it toward him so he can see it for a second and goes back to staring at it.)*

Yeah, it really turned out good, huh?

> *(The moment hangs awkwardly in the air between them.)*

PAIGE. Well, thanks for these. I don't want anything else that's in here.

JOSH. If you want something they already took, you should just talk to them.

PAIGE. I'm not gonna bother them with stupid stuff.

JOSH. You know, they're nice people.

PAIGE. When did I say / they weren't nice people?

JOSH. You have barely spoken to them through all of this.

PAIGE. Yeah, well... Where is Matty with my fucking soda?

JOSH. They said they've left you messages.

PAIGE. I've already explained to you about not calling people back. You know who else called me? *Devon.* Can you believe that?

JOSH. I saw him at the service, but I didn't talk to him. What did he want?

PAIGE. I don't know. I didn't call him back! He's the last person I'd deal with right now.

JOSH. That I get, but why won't you talk to Doug's folks? Why are you so upset with them?

PAIGE. I'm not. I'm just upset in general.

JOSH. They want us to go out there for Doug's birthday this weekend.

PAIGE. What?

JOSH. They invited / us to –

PAIGE. I can't go. I'm working.

JOSH. What about just one day?

PAIGE. I'm working.

> (**JOSH** *makes a plaintive face.*)

I'm sorry!

> (**JOSH** *slumps his shoulders and retreats.*)

What?

> (*It clicks for her.*)

You told them we'd go already, didn't you?

JOSH. No...

PAIGE. Yes, you did. That's SOO typical, you don't even ask / me if I could go.

JOSH. I just said we would try! That's it.

PAIGE. Why don't I believe you, Joshy?

JOSH. I'm telling you that's what I said. I said I would ask you, since they couldn't get in touch with you.

PAIGE. But you think we should go.

JOSH. I'm gonna go.

PAIGE. You want us to schlep all the way out to middle-of-nowhere Pennsylvania so we can awkwardly spend our dead friend's birthday with his parents? That sounds nice to you?

JOSH. Nice for them.

PAIGE. What are we gonna do there, Joshy? They gonna have cake?

JOSH. I don't know! Jesus! Look, they're never gonna get over this, okay? Can we just make this one day a little easier on them? It's only been two fucking weeks.

PAIGE. I just can't go to Pennsylvania this weekend!

JOSH. Fine!

PAIGE. I know that makes me like, the bitch of the universe, or whatever –

JOSH. No. They only offered. If we could. They'll understand.

PAIGE. I can't do it. I can't.

> (**PAIGE** *looks around the apartment trying to find something to focus on. She gets increasingly frustrated by the disappointment around her.*)

He should *be here*! Ugh, this is so fucked up. This whole fucking thing. I'm...

(She is about to burst.)

JOSH. Just say it, Paige.

PAIGE. No!

(She fights to keep it down but cannot.)

I should've been here for him. I should've stayed home. But even still, after I left, I realized I forgot my gloves, and there was a moment where I thought about coming back to get them but the elevator was out and

I couldn't... I *didn't want to* go all the way back up the fucking stairs, and the cold air made it feel like my fever went away so I just kept going. He even tried to tell me about the gloves when I was leaving, but his mouth was full of fucking cereal and I thought he'd said... "God is love."

JOSH. "God is love"?

PAIGE. Yeah.

JOSH. What's that mean?

PAIGE. I don't know! It didn't make any fucking sense to me at the time. I was running out the door, like, "Okay, whatever." But later it clicked in and right then I thought that I should come back. But I didn't. If I had just come back, I would've found him. And maybe it wouldn't have been too late. You see?

JOSH. No, I don't see. You coming back was not gonna stop what happened. It wasn't about you. That's not why he died.

PAIGE. Really? Why then?

JOSH. It was an embolism.

PAIGE. Caused by what?

JOSH. They said there was trauma.

PAIGE. Trauma that we didn't know about? How could we not know?

JOSH. I don't know. That's just how he was!

PAIGE. That's not a good enough answer.

JOSH. There's no good answer. That's just the answer.

PAIGE. Joshy. He's gone. I feel like / if I had just –

JOSH. Everyone always feels / like there's something –

PAIGE. I don't care what everyone feels! It's what I feel. What *I feel*.

JOSH. I understand that you can feel whatever you feel, but you didn't kill him and you are not responsible for what happened and you letting yourself believe –

PAIGE. You know what? Fuck this whole thing.

JOSH. No. You forgot something, and you didn't come back. So what? What if you came back, got it, and left again before anything happened to him? What's the crime then?

PAIGE. But that's not what happened.

JOSH. Right. You know, I left my charger that day. For my computer.

PAIGE. I know... We saw it.

JOSH. I was on the subway already when I realized it wasn't in my bag. Are you mad at me?

PAIGE. What? For what?

JOSH. You tell me. Is it my fault too? Are you blaming me?

(She considers her response for a moment.)

PAIGE. For a lot of things. Yeah.

*(**MATTY** re-enters from outside in a burst of energy.)*

MATTY. Cream soda!

PAIGE. Hey, what took so long?

MATTY. Well, the bodega downstairs only had two-liter bottles and since I was told that was *not* the preferred size, I had to go a few blocks down to the other bodega and then this old guy was having an argument with himself in front of the fridge with the cream soda in it, so I had to wait till he decided to argue with himself in front of the Ben and Jerry's freezer and then – woohoo! Mission accomplished! How are things going? You guys making progress?

PAIGE. Not enough. Grab the bag. Let's go pack.

JOSH. Hold up a sec, Matty. Paige is mad at me and I'd really like to know why.

PAIGE. I didn't say –

JOSH. Yes, you did. Is this why you're moving out? To punish me?

PAIGE. *God,* no.

JOSH. You never even asked me if we could look for another place. You just send me an e-mail / telling me you can't live here and moving in with Matty. Why?

PAIGE. *You* sent *me* an e-mail telling me I have to come here if I want any of Doug's stuff before they take it all. / You think that's fair to me?

JOSH. I've always been there for you and now you're just walking out on me.

PAIGE. I'm not walking out on you!

MATTY. It's just temporary.

JOSH. And this is really the most stable relationship to build on? You guys break up every couple weeks, and suddenly you're gonna be living with him? That makes sense?

PAIGE. Don't talk about my boyfriend / like he's not right in front of you.

JOSH. *Boyfriend?* He's not your boyfriend! He's a loser! You were just saying –

PAIGE. You have no fucking right to say –

JOSH. Don't tell me I don't –

MATTY. HEY!!

(*He silences them.*)

The fuck, man?

JOSH. Matty, I'm s–

MATTY. No. I'm sorry. You lost your best friend, and you're going through some messed up shit right now in your head. So let's not say anything else about it right now. I'll chalk that last bit up to a whole lotta stress. Nobody here is a loser. We're all just trying to help each other through some incredibly difficult shit. But this is your home, and clearly I'm not helping like I wanna right now, so maybe I'll just get out of here for a little while.

(To **PAIGE**.*)* Unless you need me to pack your –

PAIGE. No, it's fine. I'll meet you downstairs in a minute. I'm okay here. Thanks.

MATTY. Okay. Later, J.

> (**JOSH** *nods.* **MATTY** *exits.* **PAIGE** *turns to face* **JOSH**.*)*

PAIGE. I'm gonna go stay with Matty. He cares about me and I care about him. I'm sorry if it hurts you to hear that, but that's the truth.

JOSH. You always complain about him.

PAIGE. To you. You're my best friend. I can complain to you. / It doesn't mean I don't really like him.

JOSH. Well, I'm not your gay best friend, is all.

> *(This hits her hard.)*

PAIGE. I know that. Look, what do you want me to say?

JOSH. I want you...to think things through.

PAIGE. I have. Things will never be right here. I don't even want to look in the direction of his room right now.

> *(She wanders away from him.)*

JOSH. This was a mistake. We can't decide this right now. Everything's too raw. I just want us to stay together.

PAIGE. No. You think you do, but you don't. I'm a mess. I'm just a mess right now.

JOSH. You think I care that you're a mess? Paige, I luh–

PAIGE. Don't do this to me right now. DON'T.

JOSH. I can't say that I –

PAIGE. NO YOU CANNOT. I can't even think about it, okay? There is no room in my brain to think about it.

> *(She retreats to the upstage window. She notices a chair is tucked away, with a small throw blanket over it. As **PAIGE** pulls it out she realizes it's Doug's kitchen chair. She is alarmed.)*

What is this?

JOSH. Uh, Paige...

PAIGE. This is Dougie's chair.

JOSH. Alright, I know –

PAIGE. You kept it? Why would you keep this here?

JOSH. If you'd let / me explain for one second, I would tell you –

PAIGE. I found him in this chair...

JOSH. I'M SORRY! I couldn't get rid of it. Okay? I didn't know what to do. I couldn't look at the table anymore, so I took it all downstairs until all that was left was Doug's chair. And I just couldn't get rid of it. So I just stuck it back there and put something over it, so I didn't have to really see it.

PAIGE. So it's just gonna be there, but you don't want to acknowledge it. Sounds about right.

JOSH. What's that supposed to mean?

PAIGE. I'm gonna go get my things.

JOSH. No, come on. What the fuck, Paige?

PAIGE. There are things that Doug and I shared that I don't want to get into right now.

JOSH. *You met him through me!* When you talk now it's like I was never even part of the equation. I knew him years longer than you!

PAIGE. Well, I knew him better.

JOSH. Oh, fuck you. Don't stand there and tell me that your grief means more than everyone else's –

PAIGE. I didn't say it meant more. I said I knew him better.

JOSH. What did you know that I didn't? What are you talking about?

PAIGE. I'm talking about his feelings for you.

JOSH. What?

PAIGE. You heard me.

JOSH. Why are you doing this?

PAIGE. Someone needs to speak on his behalf.

JOSH. He was not in love with me, okay?

PAIGE. He cared for you more than anything else and you ignored certain things with him / because that's what was convenient for you.

JOSH. Doug and I – I can't believe we're having this conversation. I don't need to explain my friendship with him to you. Nothing was ever gonna happen between us. As much as I loved him, and I did, I loved him. It was never part of the equation and we were both okay with that.

PAIGE. That's such bullshit. You know it is! You took advantage of him!

JOSH. I would NEVER do that!

PAIGE. You did! Oh my God, you did!

JOSH. I don't know what the fuck you're talking about! Look, what was between you and Doug is your business and what was between me and Doug is mine. Go in your room, pack up the rest of your shit and run away.

PAIGE. I'm not running away!

JOSH. Fine. You're not running away! Just MOVE then. Have a happy life. Go be with your awesome dull-ass boyfriend, and get married – *or don't get married* – and do whatever the fuck it is you want to do with your life.

PAIGE. I can't do this now. Fuck, I'm so angry with you right now you have no idea.

JOSH. Oh, I've got a ballpark idea.

> (**PAIGE** *heads for the door.*)

Where are you going?

PAIGE. Matty's waiting for me downstairs.

JOSH. What are you doing with your room?

PAIGE. I don't know. We'll come back for my stuff tomorrow.

JOSH. I'm not taking another day off tomorrow for you!

PAIGE. I'll keep the key and do it myself! Don't call me. Don't write me. I want to hear nothing from you. You're a lying piece of shit.

JOSH. Oh, I'm the lying piece of shit? Look at yourself, Paige. Fine, go! You and Matty have an awesome life together.

> (**PAIGE** *gets to the door, stops, and looks back at* **JOSH**.)

PAIGE. I wish it was you who dropped dead instead of him.

*(She slams the door as she exits. **JOSH** stands staring at the door for a short while, totally wrecked.)*

JOSH. You and me both.

Transition

3. Dinner with Friends

(March 6, 2007 – 5:30 p.m.)

*(The table and chairs are back where they were in Scene 1. The pictures featuring **PAIGE** are gone from the walls. **DOUG** is sitting on the couch in his underwear and a D.A.R.E. T-shirt, listening to his Discman.* **JOSH** enters the apartment carrying a pizza box. He is in casual clothes with a book bag.)*

JOSH. Doug?

(He puts the pizza down on the table.)

Hey, c'mon! You said you'd help me clean!

DOUG. It looks fine in here.

JOSH. It does not look fine. Look, all this is – WILL YOU PLEASE PUT PANTS ON?

DOUG. WILL YOU PLEASE NOT YELL AT ME?

JOSH. Man, come on! I had work all day and you've been sitting here on your ass. Please help me straighten up before Paige gets here.

DOUG. I put my stuff in my room.

JOSH. Doug. Potential roommate is on her way over right now. Someone to pay a third of our rent. Therefore, she's a very important person. Please help me. And put on some fucking pants.

DOUG. I walk around like this a lot. If she's not comfortable looking at it, then this isn't gonna work out.

---

* A license to produce *The Timing of a Day* does not include a license to publicly display any branded logos or trademarked images. Licensees must acquire rights for any logos and/or images or create their own.

JOSH. Stop being an ass, okay? I can't believe you didn't wear pants all day.

DOUG. I did! I went out to get lunch, and then I took them off again.

JOSH. That's great.

(He tries to clean the couch around **DOUG**.*)*

What's all this food in the couch? Ugh!

DOUG. Which of us eats on the couch? You!

JOSH. Which of us sits right on top of it? You!

DOUG. Relax, Joshy. Here come sit down.

(He grabs at **JOSH**'s *arms and pulls him down toward the couch.* **JOSH** *tries to pull himself back with difficulty.* **DOUG** *laughs.)*

Sit with me a minute.

JOSH. Let go! C'mon, let go! We don't have time for this. There's no time to vacuum. She's gonna think we live like slobs.

DOUG. We do live like slobs.

JOSH. Well, we could try to hide it better for a good first impression.

DOUG. She should know what she's getting into right from the beginning. I believe in full disclosure.

JOSH. You spent more than twenty-six years hiding the fact that you're gay from your parents.

DOUG. That's right, and I'm not going back to the secrets and lies.

JOSH. You know, now that you're completely out of the closet, there should be room in that closet to put all your fuckin' shoes! I am gonna give the bathroom a once over.

DOUG. Yeah, I did some damage in their earlier. Sorry.

(**JOSH** *runs into the bathroom.*)

JOSH. Doug!

DOUG. Sorry!

(*The buzzer rings.* **DOUG** *doesn't acknowledge it.*)

JOSH. Wasn't that the buzzer?

DOUG. Yes.

(*Silence. It rings again.*)

JOSH. Can you answer it, please?

DOUG. Oh, I thought *you* were gonna answer it.

(**JOSH** *glares and growls.*)

Fine, I will answer it.

(**DOUG** *gets up and heads to the front door.*)

JOSH. You're gonna give her a chance, right? You said you would.

DOUG. Why wouldn't I?

JOSH. I don't know. You have a tone.

DOUG. I have a *tone*?

JOSH. Doug, *please* –

DOUG. Let me just meet her, so I can find out why you're so jumpy right now.

JOSH. I'm not acting like a –

(*There's a knock at door.* **JOSH** *jumps.*)

She's here! Now be nice!

DOUG. I'm always nice.

JOSH. Pants! C'mon.

(**DOUG** *steps into his pants, but does not pull them up as* **JOSH** *opens the door.*)

(**PAIGE** *enters, out of breath, but excited and much more fresh and happy than we've seen her before. They light up at seeing each other.*)

PAIGE. Hey!

JOSH. You made it!

PAIGE. Yeah, those five flights of stairs are no joke, dude.

(She kisses his cheek.)

Thanks for having me over.

JOSH. No prob! Sorry about the stairs. They've been fixing the elevator since Saturday. It breaks down every once in a while.

PAIGE. Well, at least I know where I'll be getting my cardio.

JOSH. It's a little messy still, so be gentle in your assessment.

PAIGE. No, it's great. I love the layout. You guys have a great space!

(*She sees* **DOUG** *finally pulling up his pants as they enter the living room.*)

JOSH. Uh, this guy finally pulling up his pants over there is Doug. Doug, Paige.

PAIGE. Hi. Nice ass!

DOUG. Thanks!

PAIGE. Dancer?

DOUG. Indeed.

PAIGE. It shows.

DOUG. This one's good. Keep it up, lady.

PAIGE. I will! So what's going on here, fellas? You didn't tell me I'd be visiting on Clothing Optional Tuesday! I didn't interrupt something between you two, did I?

JOSH. Please. He wishes.

> (**JOSH** *flashes his eyes at* **DOUG**. **DOUG** *rolls his.*)

DOUG. *Ha, ha.* I was just trying to freak him out. I hope I didn't make you feel –

> (**PAIGE** *waives him off.*)

I just enjoy torturing him.

PAIGE. So do I! We already have so much in common.

DOUG. So you want a tour of the place?

PAIGE. Sure! Point me around.

> (*He points.*)

DOUG. Kitchen over there. Living room. Back there the middle door is the bathroom and then Josh's room's on the left and mine on the right. And then last but not least we have the third bedroom over there.

PAIGE. Oh, cool!

JOSH. Nice and private. It's actually a little smaller than the other bedrooms, so we'll give you a discount on the rent.

PAIGE. $525, right?

DOUG. *Plus* utilities.

PAIGE. Nice! That's what I'm paying now and the apartment isn't nearly as nice.

DOUG. Really? Your apartment must suck.

PAIGE. Yeah, seriously. Plus, I can walk to work at the hospital from here, which is *amazing*.

DOUG. Through the park? After dark?

JOSH. Paige, can I offer you something to drink?

PAIGE. Uh, water'd be great. Thanks!

JOSH. Brita it is!

> (**JOSH** *mouths "BE NICE!" to* **DOUG** *as he makes his way back to the fridge.*)

DOUG. So Paige, where you from?

PAIGE. Well, my family's moved all over. We lived a bunch of places in Massachusetts when I was little. Then Arizona, Colorado. Lived for like two years in Florida. My parents are kinda free spirits. I came here when I got into NYU, but it wasn't really for me, so I left halfway through just to audition.

DOUG. Okay, then. You've been here long enough to know – are you a City Girl at heart? Are you here to stay?

PAIGE. To stay? I don't know. I love it, but it's hard. I think one of the nice things about living so many places is knowing there's more to the world than New York.

> (**DOUG** *makes a subtle shift in posture, which* **PAIGE** *correctly guesses means he didn't like her answer.*)

But *definitely* right now I really like the city. And I'm working for First Thought with Joshy and that's really great.

DOUG. You like First Thought?

PAIGE. Yeah, I love it! It's so much fun. At first I didn't see myself doing educational theater about sex and health and stuff, but it's great and the kids are into it. And Joshy's so great there too. He's amazing. He knows everything.

DOUG. Oh, I'm sure.

PAIGE. Were you ever in First Thought?

DOUG. No, but he's suggested it a few hundred times. You guys don't really dance though, and that's my focus.

PAIGE. We dance!

DOUG. *(Politely.)* Not really.

PAIGE. Okay...

(She mimes a knife going into her heart, moans.)

DOUG. I didn't mean it like that.

PAIGE. Yeah, you did!

DOUG. No, I just – I'd rather do full-out musicals. Where the dancing is more showcased.

PAIGE. I think it's so funny that we've never met before. Josh has been saying forever that you and I had to hang out. He thinks we're a good match.

DOUG. Well, I've never really hung out with J's First Thought friends.

PAIGE. We're an interesting bunch. Yeaaah!

*(She trills the Yeeah! and waves her finger in the air. **JOSH** copies her and they laugh at a joke **DOUG** isn't privy to.)*

DOUG. Uh, yeah.

JOSH. It's this thing one of the girls in the company does all the time during –

*(**PAIGE** feels her phone go off in her pocket.)*

PAIGE. Ugh, who's calling me? Shoot, it's my mom. Do you mind?

JOSH. No, go ahead.

PAIGE. Thanks.

(She talks into her phone.)

Hey, Ma. No, I'm here now… It was fine! It's nice – right off the subway. Yeah, nice and safe. Mom, I'm here *right now*. Hold on.

(She puts her hand over the phone.)

Sorry. This is gonna take a minute.

JOSH. No prob. Go in the open bedroom if you want. Check out the dimensions.

> *(****PAIGE**** gives a thumbs up, exits to her room. He turns to* ****DOUG****.*)*

What is wrong with you?

DOUG. Nothing's wrong with me! What's wrong with you? Did you hear her before?

JOSH. Hear what?

DOUG. She is not a city person. She's an actress who doesn't like the city! This is gonna be Danielle all over again.

JOSH. It is not gonna be Danielle!

DOUG. Yes it is. Moping around, unhappy about auditioning. She'll start thinking the city sucks and she'll bail on us like she bailed on NYU to go back to…Arizona or Florida or wherever the hell her family is now.

JOSH. Are you nuts? Paige is perfect for us! We work together. She's not gonna bail on us.

DOUG. I'd be more comfortable living with someone we *both* know and we're *both* sure of. And someone who you're not trying to screw.

JOSH. What are you talking about?

DOUG. You like this girl! And she's all over you! He's *amazing*. He knows *everything*. God, kill me now.

JOSH. Fuckwad, I have a girlfriend. And Paige also has a boyfriend, for that matter –

DOUG. Uh huh. I know you, okay? I know where this is heading.

JOSH. That's bullshit. And frankly, it's offensive to Jenna that you would say that. I'm not trying to cheat on my girlfriend!

DOUG. And does Jenna like that you want to live with Paige?

JOSH. She's not threatened by it.

DOUG. *Oh, okay.*

JOSH. C'mon, how are you gonna tell me you don't like her?

DOUG. It's not about "not liking" her / it's about you –

JOSH. Because I think you'd like her a lot, if you weren't so gung-ho about it not working out.

*(**PAIGE** re-enters, putting her phone away.)*

PAIGE. Sorry. It takes like five minutes to say goodbye to her. She never shuts up. Shall we with the pizza?

JOSH. Yes, let's!

PAIGE. Thank God, I'm starving, and the smell of the pizza is seriously shutting down everything else in my brain.

JOSH. Doug's too.

DOUG. Funny!

JOSH. Let's see what's on TV!

PAIGE. Oh, do we have to watch TV? Why don't we just sit here and eat and chat?

JOSH. At the table?

PAIGE. What, you don't eat at the table?

JOSH. I don't. Doug always wants to.

PAIGE. You have this big awesome table. What do you use it for?

JOSH. It's where we put the mail.

PAIGE. No.

JOSH. We get a lot of mail!

DOUG. I vote table. Two against one. We win.

> (**JOSH** *relents and clears the rest of the table so they can eat.* **PAIGE** *goes to sit in Doug's chair.*)

That's where I like to sit.

JOSH. They're all the same.

DOUG. I like this one. You know that.

JOSH. Yeah, what Dougie doesn't know is that I switch them around once a week and he never notices.

DOUG. You do not!

JOSH. You sure?

PAIGE. So Josh told me you guys met doing *Into The Woods* in college? I love that show. You guys were the two princes right?

DOUG. Yeah, he told you about *Leh-Leh Into The Woods*?

JOSH. *(In a throaty sexual voice.)* Leh-Leh!

DOUG. Leh-Leh!

> (*They go back and forth and laugh. Then they both tap two fingers to the side of their throats.*)

DOUG. Energy!

> (*They laugh.* **PAIGE** *is lost. She sits quietly waiting for the private joke to pass.*)

Sorry, that must seem really crazy.

PAIGE. S'okay. I just feel like we went to a strange private place just now. Who or what is Leh-Leh?

DOUG. Leh-Leh's this girl we knew in college, Lenore Knighton, she was a little weird.

JOSH. Try bat-shit crazy.

DOUG. Okay, yeah. Amazing soprano, but out of her mind. Josh called her Leh-Leh and started doing it in this weird voice 'cause he's a moron.

> (*He starts laughing.*)

It just kinda stuck. It always makes me think of her and laugh.

JOSH. She used to go around tapping her neck and saying, "Energy!" Because she said it released endorphins. She was a lot. And of course she had this huge stupid crush on me.

DOUG. Yeah, she was Cinderella. Josh was her prince. She wanted their relationship to be very "method." Josh didn't want anything to do with her.

PAIGE. Was she pretty?

JOSH. Not enough to make up for the crazy. I made sure Doug was always around me so Leh-Leh couldn't get me alone. That's how we became friends.

PAIGE. Aww, so no scandalous cast hookup for you then, Joshy?

> (**JOSH** *and* **DOUG** *exchange a glance.*)

JOSH. Well, not for me…

DOUG. Uh, excuse me...

PAIGE. What? Tell me!

JOSH. During the run of *Leh-Leh Into the Woods* it became a hot topic that Doug – who had previously not been out to anyone – had sex *in the theater* with this kid Patrick who was also in the show.

PAIGE. REALLY?

DOUG. No!

PAIGE. Wait, who'd Patrick play?

JOSH. The COW!

PAIGE. Milky White...

JOSH. Yeah – but see, it was Doug's *first time*, and he told me about it, but he didn't want anyone else to know. So, of course, Patrick then told everyone.

PAIGE. Nooo.

DOUG. That's not even right, ass, and you know it.

JOSH. It is! What'd I get wrong?

DOUG. It was *not* in the theater.

JOSH. I don't know about that...

DOUG. Omigod, it was in his dorm room one night after rehearsal. He told people it was in the theater. I guess that sounded cooler. Why would I lie about it? It doesn't make any difference now!

JOSH. Well, it sure made a difference back then. Dougie was pretty upset about it.

DOUG. Yeah, and I've had trust issues ever since! The end! You're unbelievable.

PAIGE. Wow. So that's how you got outed, huh?

DOUG. Yeah, well, at school, but nobody cared there. I actually just told my parents a couple weeks ago.

PAIGE. No way!

DOUG. Yeah, they're kind of Uber-Catholic Pennsylvania kind of people. It's not something we'd just talk about.

JOSH. I'm surprised Patrick never e-mailed them about it, to be honest.

PAIGE. What made you finally tell them?

DOUG. It was just time. I'm seeing someone right now and we've been together for a long time.

PAIGE. Ooh, tell me about him!

DOUG. Uh, well, his name is Devon. He's great. I like him a lot. And it reached a point where I didn't want to keep him from them anymore.

PAIGE. So how'd it go?

DOUG. Not so awesome. They were supposed to come up for a dance show I did last week, and they didn't make it. They said it was weather related. They are gonna come up for another thing though in two weeks and they agreed to meet Devon then.

PAIGE. Good! I want to meet him too! Josh didn't tell me about him.

DOUG. No? Josh doesn't like him.

JOSH. That's not true.

DOUG. He beat Josh at Cranium once and Josh hasn't forgiven him. This one's very competitive at board games.

JOSH. That's not why.

DOUG. No one's good enough, I guess.

PAIGE. Aww, you boys are so cute. My two princes!

JOSH. Oh, please. Now TV time?

DOUG. Before that, I'd like to speak to Paige one-on-one. If you don't mind.

JOSH. I have to actually leave the room?

DOUG. Just for a sec, 'kay?

JOSH. But I –

(**PAIGE** *gives* **JOSH** *a reassuring smile.*)

Okay. I will wait in my room and in no way have my ear against the door to eavesdrop.

PAIGE. Josh, shoo! Don't be a baby. Oh, look he's all wounded. Get lost!

(They all chuckle. **JOSH** *exits.* **DOUG** *turns to* **PAIGE.***)*

DOUG. So.

PAIGE. So! What's up?

DOUG. Okay, don't get me wrong, you seem great. Easy to talk to. I just – I have some concerns…

PAIGE. Like what?

DOUG. Okay, how do I put this? You and Josh have a very…unique friendship.

PAIGE. We do?

DOUG. Don't you?

PAIGE. No.

DOUG. There's no…attraction there?

PAIGE. Ohhh… Well, when we first met he and I discussed dating for like, two seconds, but then we both realized that would be bad cuz we'd kill each other, so it's never been an issue since then. We work great as friends. Just friends. And I have a boyfriend. Maybe Josh didn't tell you.

DOUG. He did…

PAIGE. And Josh is with Jenna, so…?

DOUG. So…

>   *(He exhales, at a loss. **PAIGE** leans in and takes his hand. Her tone shifts, her lightness falls.)*

PAIGE. Doug, I really need this right now. My current place is not an option anymore. I need to be out by the end of next week. If you'd seen the other shit-holes I've seen – this is by FAR my best bet. We can make it work. I promise you no weirdness with Josh.

DOUG. You promise?

PAIGE. Cross my heart.

>   *(She does, and smiles. He smiles back.)*

DOUG. Just so you know? I refuse to live by a "chore wheel." I see any attempt to organize one on the door to the fridge and you're out on your ass.

PAIGE. *(She screams with delight.)* Thank you!

>   *(**JOSH** calls out from his room.)*

JOSH. This sounds like good news! Can I come out now?

DOUG. Yes, come on out!

JOSH. So we're settled?

>   *(**DOUG** nods with reluctant approval.)*

PAIGE. Yeah and now that I know that I'm in. I brought this!

>   *(She pulls a bottle of wine out of her bag.)*

DOUG. Wine! Yes!

PAIGE. It's cheap, but it's good.

JOSH. That's how we like it around here. Were we not gonna get the wine if we said no?

PAIGE. Hell no! I'd be drinking this whole thing by myself on the way home in that case.

JOSH. I'll get the cork out.

(He goes to the kitchen with the bottle.)

DOUG. So when can you move in?

PAIGE. I have to check with my friend who has a van, but I'm thinking this weekend looks good?

DOUG. This weekend looks good.

JOSH. Okay, here's the wine. Are we making a toast?

DOUG. I'll do it.

PAIGE. Oh, please do.

*(****DOUG*** *thinks for a moment to get the wording right.)*

DOUG. *(In the style of a Golden Age Hollywood actress.)* "It's a funny thing, time.

*(****JOSH*** *rolls his eyes, but* ***PAIGE*** *catches the reference right away.)*

In the present, you're always the oldest you've ever been. Sometimes that makes you *feel* old, even when you're young and just making choices. It's only when you look back that you realize...you were practically a baby. Here's to us, a long time from now, laughing about today and about how old we *thought* we were."

PAIGE. Cheers!

(They clink glasses and drink.)

JOSH. Is that from something?

DOUG. Yes. It's –

PAIGE. *Unapologetically Jane!*

DOUG. You do *not* know / that movie.

PAIGE. How do *you* know that movie? / I don't know anyone else who –

DOUG. I own that movie on VHS and DVD.

PAIGE. Stop. "You love a heart forged in fire and brimstone!"

DOUG. "Tall?"

PAIGE & DOUG. "You think *you're* tall?"

DOUG. "Give me back my money, Jane!"

PAIGE. "Give me back my life!"

> *(They laugh and clink their glasses together again.)*

JOSH. Um, okay then. Cheers.

Transition

4. The Loneliness of Evening

(July 10, 2007 – 8:30 p.m.)

*(**DOUG** is in the apartment by himself. He is sitting on the floor of the bathroom with his headphones on, staring at the ceiling. **PAIGE** comes in the apartment with a bag of groceries. She kicks the door shut behind her and **DOUG** hears it and gets up.)*

DOUG. Hey...

PAIGE. Hey! You're alone in the house and wearing pants? What's the occasion?

DOUG. I dunno. Do you know where Josh is?

PAIGE. Yeah, he went to see Jenna after work... Those two are so weird.

DOUG. What do you mean?

PAIGE. Something's up with them. He flinches every time someone mentions her. I don't think he even realizes. Dude has no poker face.

*(She sees **DOUG** is upset.)*

What's wrong?

DOUG. Nothing. I was just hoping to talk to Josh. He's not picking up his phone.

PAIGE. Maybe he's on the subway. What's wrong? Talk to me.

DOUG. S'okay... I have a headache. I'm gonna go lie down in my room for a while.

PAIGE. Okay.

*(**DOUG** exits to his room. **PAIGE** continues to put groceries away. After a moment **DOUG** comes back in.)*

DOUG. Okay, you'll listen? Without judging?

PAIGE. Of course! What's going on?

DOUG. Devon sorta disappeared. I think maybe he left me.

PAIGE. Oh no! Since when?

DOUG. It's been about...six weeks.

PAIGE. Six *weeks*? Dougie, why didn't you say something sooner?

DOUG. I kept thinking I'd hear from him and then I felt stupid for waiting so long.

PAIGE. Wait, is he GONE gone? Did he leave the city?

DOUG. No, people have seen him. I just haven't seen him.

PAIGE. Look, just tell me what happened.

DOUG. The last time I saw him was back in June, that weekend we went to the Bronx Zoo? We had a great time. I stayed over at his place that night. The sex was good. He seemed happy. I was really happy. Then when I woke up on Sunday... I don't know. He seemed weird. I thought maybe he was just in a mood... He had an early shift at the restaurant, so we left his place together. We said goodbye at the subway, he gave me a kiss and said "I love you." I said, "I love you too." He turned and walked away and that was the last time I saw him.

PAIGE. Have you talked to him?

DOUG. No. I sent him texts and voicemails and e-mails. At first they were normal and then they got more panicked. I thought something horrible could've happened to him. How was I gonna know? So then I went to the restaurant to make sure he'd been there.

PAIGE. Had he?

DOUG. Yeah, but his boss was a total dick and treated me like I was some stalker or something. Told me he didn't like people coming in bothering his staff with "personal problems." And then he laughed at me, like it was some joke. I just left. I haven't been back.

PAIGE. Okay, putting that asshole aside for a moment, there's something here I'm not getting. Doug, there've been dozens of times in the past couple weeks that you've told me you were going out with Devon. Where've you been going?

DOUG. Sometimes I'd go to his building and wait outside to see if I'd catch him coming in or out. But then I stopped, 'cause I really did feel like a stalker. So I mostly just kinda walked in the park... I know how pathetic it sounds. I just couldn't understand what happened. A week after I went to the restaurant, Devon texted me saying he needed space and was dealing with shit, and I was not helping the situation by crowding him. I sent him a message back just asking if he wanted to end things completely. No response. And that's been it for... almost a month now.

PAIGE. I can't believe I didn't notice he hasn't been here in that long!

DOUG. Yeah, well...

PAIGE. You could've told us, Dougie... Wait, does Josh know? Is that why you're looking for him?

DOUG. No, he doesn't know. I wanted to fix things myself. I thought if I told you guys, you'd be against him and that would make everything harder.

PAIGE. Maybe he deserves to have people against him! I mean, what the fuck? He can't treat you that way! That's bullshit.

DOUG. No, no. I don't want you getting mad at him. I just want to know what's going on. A friend of Jenna's works at Blondie's with him, so I was gonna see if maybe Jenna could talk to her friend and see if he's in trouble...or if he's seeing someone else, I don't know. I just need answers before I go out of my mind here.

PAIGE. Doug, if this is how Devon's treating you, then you need to walk away. This is bullshit. I know you've invested a lot in this guy, I do, but you hanging on is not gonna lead you anywhere good.

DOUG. But I need to know why.

PAIGE. Sometimes there is no why. The why is that the guy's an asshole.

DOUG. But he's not.

PAIGE. Well, he's definitely a coward. If he lost interest, then he should just fucking tell you instead of running away and hiding. I mean, it's like with Greg and me last month. Things were fine and then one day we just lost that spark. We both knew it, but at least we talked about it before he bounced. Devon should've had the guts to say something to you. That's shitty.

DOUG. It wasn't like that though. Everything was fine... I introduced him to my *parents*. They *liked* him. God, what am I supposed to tell them now? They're not gonna understand 'cause I don't even understand. I told him I *loved* him... I'm in love with him.

(**PAIGE** *considers him for a moment.*)

PAIGE. Is Devon the first person you've been in love with?

DOUG. He's the first person I've said it to.

(*They sit for a moment quietly.*)

I keep replaying that day in my head, 'cause I must've done something or said something that –

PAIGE. No. You're not blaming yourself for this guy dicking you around.

(**PAIGE** *gets up and walks toward the front door.*)

DOUG. Where are you going?

PAIGE. To the restaurant. I'm going to talk to him.

DOUG. No, don't. He'll think I sent you!

PAIGE. Trust me. He won't see me coming before it's too late.

DOUG. Paige...

PAIGE. You want answers, so...

DOUG. You're going to punch him, aren't you?

PAIGE. Maybe. No one fucking ABANDONS my roommate and then walks away as if nothing happened.

DOUG. I don't even know if he's there now, just wait for –

*(Keys can be heard in the door. **JOSH** enters looking like he's been through the ringer.)*

PAIGE. Josh... What's wrong?

JOSH. DUMPED.

DOUG. What?

JOSH. Would a full sentence make it clearer? I have been dumped.

PAIGE. No way.

JOSH. Oh, yes way.

PAIGE. This is... I don't believe this.

DOUG. For real? Buddy, what happened?

JOSH. Apparently, Jenna can't tell where we are heading. She's been worrying about it for a while and thinks we don't have the same goals. She's met someone.

PAIGE. Get the fuck out.

JOSH. Yeah. She swears I don't know him. Lucky him. Apparently, he works in *finance.* According to Jenna, I've stopped thinking about my *future*, I'm *stagnating* at my job, and I don't have the *ambition* needed to get myself to the next level.

PAIGE. What the fuck is she – *ambition*? She's a Kaplan tutor! Who is she to talk about other people's career planning?

JOSH. That's what she said. If you've never had someone you love list all the things you fear about yourself as reasons for why they're leaving you, I *highly* recommend it. Oh, it's fantastic.

DOUG. I can't believe she said that.

PAIGE. I can't believe this is all happening at once.

JOSH. What's all at once?

> (**PAIGE** *looks at* **DOUG**, *who lets out a long breath.*)

DOUG. Devon and I are over.

JOSH. What? What the hell happened?

DOUG. I don't know. He…doesn't want to be with me. I guess that's all there is to it, really.

JOSH. This happened today?

DOUG. It's been heading there for a while, I guess. But yeah.

JOSH. Unbelievable. Come here, man.

> (**JOSH** *hugs* **DOUG**. **DOUG** *crumples a little.* **JOSH** *tears up as well. As they hug,* **PAIGE** *runs to the fridge and gets beers.* **DOUG** *pulls away.*)

DOUG. Okay, okay.

JOSH. I guess bad shit does come in threes. Relationship dominoes –

> (*He points to* **PAIGE**, **DOUG**, *and then himself.*)

Bing, Bang, Boom… I just didn't expect this at all right now.

PAIGE. Look, I just got some beer and snacks at the bodega. We are gonna sit here and drink and eat until we're fatties, and talk shit about our exes for the rest of the night. Crying is banned. If anyone feels like a cry is coming on, we'll all get up and dance around to "Since U Been Gone" on my CD player. Agreed?

JOSH. This sucks.

PAIGE. Agreed. Relationships are useless. We just gotta find random hot people and have lots of sex. We're all good-looking and now we're all suddenly single. We'll go out together. You guys can be my wingmen. Seriously. Look, I'm happy I don't have anyone serious in my life. I don't *want* anyone serious in my life. We should focus on doing the things we want to do without having to worrying about someone else's shitty expectations. You know? Otherwise you start making compromises with yourself and it's –

(**JOSH** *gets up.*)

What's up?

JOSH. I'm gonna go in my room for a while.

PAIGE. No! Stay!

DOUG. C'mon, man.

JOSH. I'll be back. I just want a minute to breathe and check my e-mail, okay? Thanks for the beer.

(**JOSH** *exits to his room.*)

PAIGE. What did I say?

DOUG. Just give him a minute. I think he might want to cry and his falsetto's not so great for Clarkson.

PAIGE. Okay... I'm really sorry about Devon.

DOUG. Don't go out and punch him, okay? I'd like to be able to know I can tell you these kinda things without you immediately jumping to violence.

PAIGE. But it's so effective!

(**DOUG** *gives her a look.*)

Fine. If it means I have your confidence. I will refrain from violence.

DOUG. Thanks... Can I ask you a question?

PAIGE. Sure. Whatever.

DOUG. Have you ever had your heart, like, really broken?

PAIGE. Yeah. Once.

DOUG. How long did it take to get over it?

PAIGE. Who says I'm over it?

(*She smirks.*)

We're gonna be fine. All three of us. Tomorrow's a new day and time heals all wounds.

(*She clinks her beer bottle with his.*)

DOUG. I think it's time for you to cue up Ms. Clarkson.

Transition

5. Stumbling Through the Dark

(July 8, 2008 – 11:45 p.m.)

(The apartment is in post–Game Night messiness. The table has several board games on it, along with Doug's Discman. Lots of empty wine bottles, liquor bottles, and beer cans are scattered around the living space. Some pictures of **PAIGE** *have been restored to the wall.* **DOUG** *and* **JOSH** *occupy the couch.* **MATTY** *is in the armchair.* **PAIGE** *is at the door saying goodbye to the last of the guests who are leaving for the night. They've all been drinking quite a bit,* **JOSH** *more than anyone, which is unusual for him.)*

(Note: **JOSH** *and* **PAIGE** *should step on each other's lines as often as possible.)*

PAIGE. Okay, get home safe, babes! Mwah!

> *(She shuts the door and turns back to the guys.)*

Good Game Night, fellas!

> *(She runs and high fives* **MATTY** *and* **DOUG**.*)*

DOUG. You too, lady.

PAIGE. Better luck next time, Joshy.

JOSH. You guys cheated.

PAIGE. How did we cheat?

JOSH. You put random-ass people in Celebrity.

PAIGE. So? That's not cheating!

JOSH. Celeste Holmes? A celebrity. Really?

PAIGE. Celeste *Holm*. Golden Age Hollywood. People on our team knew her.

MATTY. I didn't know that one either, man.

PAIGE. Don't defend him being a sore loser. He takes it too seriously.

JOSH. The teams weren't fair.

PAIGE. We chose teams at random!

JOSH. Everyone knows you two share a pop-culture brain. / You should've each been team captains to make it even.

PAIGE. You and Doug are MUCH worse about crazy mind meld stuff than him and me which is why everyone else insisted you guys be split up.

JOSH. *(To* **DOUG**.*)* You have nothing to add?

DOUG. I just think it's nice to be thought of as such a power player.

    (He goes to the bar area to get more wine.)

JOSH. Well you guys didn't get stuck with *Amber*.

    (The **OTHERS** *laugh.)*

PAIGE. That's true!

MATTY. I can't believe it took her forty-five seconds to come up with a verbal clue for *Harry Potter*!

PAIGE. I know! She's seen the movies...

JOSH. Doug, fix me a drink with all our remaining vodka, please?

DOUG. 'Kay.

MATTY. Anyone want to do a tequila shot with me?

PAIGE. Me! Doug?

DOUG. I'm good with my wine.

MATTY. Josh?

JOSH. Nah.

PAIGE. Okay, just you and me. Let's go! Yeaaah!

> *(They go back to the kitchen area to get the tequila. **JOSH** watches them, ruefully. **DOUG** returns with Josh's drink.)*

JOSH. *Yeaaah!* I'm so glad she decided to invite *that guy* over.

DOUG. Matty's kinda cool.

JOSH. She met him like a week ago and he's coming to Game Night? Isn't that a little strange?

DOUG. It gave us an even number of people for teams.

JOSH. Yeah, well I don't think Matty got the memo that the party's over. Why is he still here?

DOUG. What do you mean, "Why"?

JOSH. What do *you* mean, "What do I mean"? You think he's staying over?

> *(**DOUG** doesn't answer. **MATTY** and **PAIGE** down their shots and cheer.)*

Great.

> *(**JOSH** gulps downs his drink. **MATTY** returns to the armchair. **PAIGE** sits in his lap. **JOSH** isn't pleased.)*

MATTY. Josh, do you have work tomorrow?

JOSH. No, I start my new job next week.

MATTY. Oh, that's right. You said that earlier. With the... analyzing.

JOSH. Advertising.

MATTY. That's right! That's right. What are you doing with them?

JOSH. It's mostly administrative.

DOUG. It pays really well though and it's got a creative aspect to it too. And career mobility.

JOSH. I guess.

DOUG. It does, and full benefits and everything.

MATTY. Sweet. I wish I had insurance. My roommate got appendicitis last fall and he didn't have insurance and he totally got fucked with the bills. He had to be in there for a couple days. It was like 15,000 dollars.

PAIGE. That's really depressing.

MATTY. Josh's got the right idea to get in some place that covers him.

PAIGE. Josh is selling out.

DOUG. *Hey.*

PAIGE. What? I can't have an opinion?

JOSH. She's upset I'm leaving First Thought.

PAIGE. You're leaving me there with all the crazies!

JOSH. You don't have to stay there, you can go too.

PAIGE. No. I like the work. *It means something.*

JOSH. I *know.*

(*To* **MATTY**.) I just need something new. It's been a couple years.

MATTY. Nothing wrong with that.

(*To* **PAIGE**.) Josh is just the first of us to be an actual adult and get a job.

JOSH. Awesome.

PAIGE. You are less cute when you are not agreeing with me.

MATTY. Well, then let me shut up.

>(**JOSH** *chugs his drink finishing it off. He gets up.*)

JOSH. I'm gonna go check my e-mail.

PAIGE. Everyone we know was here tonight, who's gonna have written to you?

JOSH. I'm just gonna check my fucking e-mail! Jeez.

>(*He exits. The* **OTHERS** *drunkenly stifle laughs through the tension.*)

MATTY. Well, I'm just gonna go use the restroom...and then I guess I should head out.

PAIGE. Oh...okay.

>(**PAIGE** *doesn't move from his lap.*)

MATTY. Can I get up?

PAIGE. Sure...

>(*Again she waits to move, but finally does.* **MATTY** *smiles and exits into the bathroom.*)

DOUG. What're you doin'?

PAIGE. Nothing. What're you doing?

DOUG. Paige...

PAIGE. *Doug...*

DOUG. You're being kinda tough on him, don't you think? You've been needling him all night –

PAIGE. What're you talking about? I haven't –

DOUG. *Yes.* Lotsa little digs and comments.

>(**PAIGE** *starts to straighten up the room up.*)

PAIGE.   Don't put it all on me. He's pissing me off. Everything's about his stupid job lately. I'm just done hearing about it.

(She points to the wine.)

You want me to leave this here?

DOUG. Yeah, I might have some more.

(They organize the kitchen.)

PAIGE. I don't get what his problem is anyway.

DOUG. He's lonely. I think it's hard for him to –

PAIGE. No, it's not hard for him. He makes it hard for himself. You're way overprotective of him.

DOUG. I am not.

PAIGE. Look, I know you've got some awesome male bonding-solidarity thing going on as a result of your simultaneous dumpage? But that was forever ago. Time to MOVE ON. You did! Why can't he? What's his problem?

*(**MATTY** re-enters from bathroom.)*

MATTY. Okay, well maybe I should find my shoes and my jacket and head out.

DOUG. So soon, Matty?

MATTY. Ha! I know right? Last guest standing. I'll get out of here so you can have some peace.

PAIGE. Wait! Come over here I want to ask you something.

*(**PAIGE** leads **MATTY** over to the kitchen.)*

MATTY. What's up?

*(**PAIGE** pulls **MATTY** close. We can't hear what she's saying to him, but **MATTY** likes what*

he's hearing. He looks at **PAIGE** *as if to ask if she's serious.* **PAIGE** *leans in and kisses him. They start making out,* **DOUG** *pretends to not notice from the couch, awkwardly fidgeting with his Discman.* **JOSH** *walks in from his room immediately sees what is going on and banks back into the bathroom. He slams the door, and* **PAIGE** *and* **MATTY** *come up for air.)*

PAIGE. Okay?

MATTY. Okay! Yeah, definitely.

PAIGE. Okay!

MATTY. Okay!

PAIGE. Doug, I think we're gonna turn in for the night.

DOUG. *(Flat.)* Okay.

PAIGE. Have a good night!

DOUG. You too, guys.

MATTY. Yeah, nice meeting you tonight!

DOUG. Mmhmm. Paige? Music?

PAIGE. Yeah, no problem. I'll put something on.

DOUG. Goodniiiight.

PAIGE. Goodniiiight. Tell Josh I said goodnight.

DOUG. Okay...

(**PAIGE** *and* **MATTY** *exit to her room and close the door.* **JOSH** *opens the bathroom door.)*

You can come out now. It's safe.

JOSH. Great. So that's happening, huh?

DOUG. Yup.

(Picks up Josh's glass to offer it to him.)

DOUG. Figured we'd kill the bottle before turning in.

> (**JOSH** *walks past him and goes and does a shot instead.*)

JOSH. Well, fine. I guess that's... Is she putting some music on at least?

DOUG. Supposed to, but I don't think she's gonna remember. Let's put something on out here.

JOSH. Yes, mix CD to the rescue.

> (*He goes over to the CD player.*)

I will take "Game Night Mix" out, and..."Great Adventure Mix '07"?

DOUG. Kick ass.

> (**JOSH** *puts the CD on. Perhaps "We're Alright" by Supergrass plays.*[*])

This is a good one.

JOSH. Yup, good noise disruption music.

> (**MATTY** *enters from Paige's room looking slightly more disheveled than when he entered. He's looking at* **JOSH** *which makes* **JOSH** *very tense.*)

'Sup Matty?

MATTY. Hey, Josh. Um, I'm actually staying over and um, I wasn't really planning to stay originally and I was wondering if I could have...

JOSH. What? Pajamas?

---

* A license to produce *The Timing of a Day* does not include a performance license for any third-party or copyrighted music. Licensees should create an original composition or use music in the public domain. For further information, please see the Music and Third-Party Materials Use Note on page iii.

MATTY. Well, *no*. Condoms.

JOSH. OH…

MATTY. Yeah, Paige thought she had some from work, but she gave them all out or something? I don't know. I just kinda need some and she thought you might have some. Do you?

JOSH. Paige told you to ask me for condoms?

MATTY. Uh, yeah. She thought you'd have some from the workshops? Did I get it wrong?

JOSH. No, that's right. I mean, I'm not using them anytime soon, so yeah, let me get you some of my "work condoms."

MATTY. Thanks, dude. I really appreciate it.

JOSH. Uh huh.

> (*He goes over to a bag in the far side of the room, rifles through it, pulls out a condom.*)

Here's one.

> (*He brings it to* **MATTY**.)

MATTY. Could I actually grab a couple?

> (**JOSH** *glares, but goes back to bag and gets a few more.*)

JOSH. You know double-bagging breaks down the latex…

MATTY. One at a time. Got it!

> (**JOSH** *hands over the condoms.*)

Thanks! I owe you one.

JOSH. Please, don't mention it.

> (**MATTY** *exits back into Paige's room.*)

Ever. I fucking *hate* that kid.

DOUG. That was painful.

(**JOSH** *goes to get himself another drink.*)

JOSH. She had to ask him to ask me, didn't she? "Hey! Josh has a whole supply he isn't using! Why don't you go ask him?" You heard him. It wasn't like she said, "Go ask the guys." She just wanted to twist it in my face. That's shitty.

DOUG. I don't think she meant that. She's had a lot to drink. She's in a non-thinking place.

JOSH. Yeah? Sounds good to me.

(*He throws back a shot, heads over to* **DOUG**.)

This really sucks man. We shouldn't be the guys rejected at the end of the night.

DOUG. It's just a dry patch.

JOSH. Dry patch? Try a fucking drought in the motherfucking Mojave desert.

DOUG. It's not that bad.

JOSH. It's been over a year for me, Doug. A year.

DOUG. Okay, well...

JOSH. I'm stuck. I know I'm just sitting around, waiting...

DOUG. Well, you're never gonna get anything you don't ask for. Put yourself out there more.

JOSH. I don't want to put myself out there. I want to put myself in *there.*

(*He swings an arm toward Paige's room.*)

This sucks.

DOUG. If you wanted to date her, you shouldn't have asked her to move in.

JOSH. But I didn't know that at the time!

DOUG. C'mon man. Cut the shit. You two are just friends now. She doesn't see you that way anymore.

JOSH. Did she tell you that? You know that for sure?

DOUG. I know that because she is in there with him and not you.

JOSH. You're right. Fuck me… She's the one, Doug. The one that got away.

DOUG. Oh, GOD. I am cutting you off.

JOSH. No, I'm serious. I missed my chance. Now I'm alone.

DOUG. Hello? I'm right here.

JOSH. Yeah, but you'll leave one day and then it will just be me here. Alone.

DOUG. No way.

JOSH. YES.

(He points to the wine.)

Some of that, please. Fill 'er up.

*(**DOUG** pours wine for **JOSH**.)*

DOUG. We can stay here alone together. I'll teach you to knit and do yoga and we can play cards and watch reality TV. 'Kay?

JOSH. C'mon man. You are smart. Funny. You're in great shape. You've got…fun hair. Good teeth –

DOUG. I like this conversation now. Keep going.

JOSH. You're talented. You're *Equity*! You're funny. Did I already say funny?

DOUG. Yeah, you did.

JOSH. Well, you are funny. Some dude's gonna…grab you up.

DOUG. You are DRUNK!

JOSH. No!

DOUG. Yeah, you are.

JOSH. You're the one who's drunk! I can totally see it in your face.

DOUG. Maybe, I am, but not like you. And I don't think anyone ever counted "Equity" as one of my selling points. Thanks.

JOSH. You know another thing? I never –

(He spills wine all over his shirt.)

Fuck. Me.

*(**DOUG** laughs.)*

DOUG. You are druuuuunk.

JOSH. I ruined my shirt! I ruined it. Goddamn. I love this shirt.

DOUG. You can get it cleaned.

JOSH. Why'd you have to fill my glass so high?

DOUG. *(Still laughing.)* You said fill 'er up!

JOSH. Yeah, but that was too high!

DOUG. Fine, blame me. It's my fault. But you've definitely had enough for tonight. Go change.

JOSH. I will.

*(**JOSH** exits to his room. **DOUG** laughs to himself and drinks more from his glass. **JOSH** comes in wearing the D.A.R.E. T-shirt.)*

DOUG. That's mine.

JOSH. Not anymore.

DOUG. You can't just take my clothes!

JOSH. Yeah, I can, if I do laundry.

DOUG. When do you do my laundry? Never!

JOSH. I was picking up clothes around the common areas. Perhaps the shirt was carelessly thrown around, and now it's mine.

DOUG. I want my shirt back.

JOSH. You want me to take it off?

DOUG. Yeah, baby. Strip for me.

JOSH. Alright then.

> (**JOSH** *starts to do a little circle move with his hips. Drunkenly, he can't get the shirt over his head.* **DOUG** *doubles over with laughter at the sight.)*

Shut up. Stop laughing!

DOUG. You look ridiculous! This is why you haven't had sex in a year!

JOSH. Shut up! Loser!

> (**JOSH** *pulls the shirt off over his head. He throws it in* **DOUG**'s *face, and jumps on the couch. He starts playfully punching* **DOUG**.)

DOUG. Ow! Ow! Alright! Alright!

JOSH. Take it back!

DOUG. I take it back! I take it back! It's not the reason.

> (**JOSH** *flumps down next to* **DOUG**. *He is barely awake. His head is slumped back against the couch.)*

JOSH. I'm a loser.

DOUG. No!

JOSH. Yeah, I am. I can't make anything happen. I try to do what I love and one girl dumps me. I try to make a move for myself and the next girl won't look at me. I can't get it right. I'm sick of having feelings for someone who won't even look at me.

(He looks over at **DOUG**.*)*

You think it's stupid. Fine.

DOUG. No. I just think it's all the alcohol talking.

JOSH. No, it's me talking!

DOUG. Alright, look. You've got a great new job. You're gonna be awesome at it. You'll meet someone there to hook up with. No pity parties.

JOSH. I just feel like if someone…liked me, if they saw something, then I'd know I was worth something again. God, that's so stupid…

DOUG. I know someone you're worth something to… LEH-LEH!

(They both start laughing.)

JOSH. No!

DOUG. Oh yeah, baby. We're calling her up right now. Where's my phone?

JOSH. You don't have her fucking number!

DOUG. Yeah, I do. She gave it in case of Josh Sex Emergencies. Leh-Leh, come on over. It is TIIIME!

(He wraps his arm around **JOSH***'s head, taps* **JOSH***'s neck, Leh-Leh style.)*

Better boost up, boy!

JOSH. You're such a dick.

DOUG. I bet that's her ringtone Leh-leh. Leh-leh leh-leh leh-leh!

(*They both laugh hard and drunk at this.*)

JOSH. Fuckin' Leh-Leh! Thanks for making me laugh, D.

DOUG. Anytime.

> (**JOSH** *pats* **DOUG**'s *leg and leaves his hand there, absently rubbing* **DOUG**'s *thigh. His eyes are closed.* **DOUG** *stares at his friend for a long moment.* **JOSH** *looks vulnerable and hurt.* **DOUG** *pushes some hair out of* **JOSH**'s *face with care, and smiles. He leans in and kisses* **JOSH** *softly on his temple and nuzzles him. It is loving and intimate.* **JOSH**'s *eyes flick open. The two* **FRIENDS** *consider each other, from very different places.*)

JOSH. Doug...are you a good kisser?

DOUG. (*Unprepared.*) Maybe...

> (**JOSH** *leans in to* **DOUG** *and kisses him on the mouth.* **DOUG** *is confused, but reciprocates.* **DOUG** *puts his hand on* **JOSH**'s *chest.* **JOSH** *guides it down to his crotch. Their chests press together. They grope at each other briefly.* **JOSH** *breaks it off and looks at* **DOUG**. **DOUG** *thinks they are playing and leans in again, but* **JOSH** *pushes him back.* **DOUG** *tries again.* **JOSH** *finally finds his words.*)

JOSH. (*Quietly.*) I don't want you.

> (**DOUG** *immediately breaks off, shocked at having misread the situation. The energy between them shifts. Suddenly* **DOUG** *is very sober again.*)

JOSH. I don't want you...

DOUG. I...know that.

JOSH. What just happened?

DOUG. I – I don't know. I...

JOSH. ...Do you want to be with me?

DOUG. I... No, I really don't. I thought / it was just –

JOSH. Wait, what? What did you just say?

DOUG. Oh. Wow. You are really drunk.

JOSH. But you were all – with the nuzzling and... What's going on here? Tell me the truth.

DOUG. Look, we just had too much to drink. I had this stupid thought –

(**JOSH** *groans, rubs his head.*)

– for like a second. You looked so – and then you just – it was stupid.

JOSH. Gimme back my shirt.

(**DOUG** *throws it to him from the couch. He puts it back on.*)

S'MY shirt.

(**JOSH** *staggers aimlessly toward the kitchen table. Leans on a chair.*)

DOUG. How you doing, you okay?

JOSH. I don't know...

(*The following is said very seriously, but it's drunk talk.*)

You're there...but how can I possibly *know* that? First there's nothing. But there's something done to nothing which puts something in its place. And then it's something so there's no nothing.

DOUG. That was a lot of words in search of a sentence.

JOSH. Shut up! Shut it. You are messy. You shouldn't have kissed me.

DOUG. *I* shouldn't have kissed *you*?

JOSH. Yeah, you started it!

(Drunkenly patronizing.) Doug, you and I... We are not meant to be lovers.

DOUG. That's not what that was about. Okay? It's just... We were on the couch and I got this idea that... I just thought I'd kiss it and make it all better. I know that sounds... I don't know how it sounds. I thought, I would kiss it and make it better. Just like this one comforting thing as you were next to me and we were both... I didn't mean to send you a different signal. I'm sorry.

(**JOSH** *moves back closer to him.*)

JOSH. Kiss it and make it better?

DOUG. Yeah. *Ohhh, let me kiss it and make it better.* That's what came into my head. Okay?

(**JOSH** *sits back down on the couch next to* **DOUG**.)

JOSH. Okay...

(**JOSH** *leans into* **DOUG** *led by his mouth. His body thinks kissing would feel good but his brain is totally checked out.* **DOUG** *watches him, but leans back.*)

DOUG. Josh...

> *(Their faces get closer. There's a moment where it seems they might fall back into kissing again. Then something inside Paige's room gets knocked over loudly and we hear* **PAIGE** *and* **MATTY** *laugh.* **JOSH** *swings his head around to look toward her door. Moment over.)*

JOSH. Great. That's *awesome*. Fuck so hard you bring the whole building down! Why is my life like this? I can't get anything to work right! This is all wrong. All of it.

DOUG. I'm sorry.

JOSH. For what? For hiding your feelings from me? Aaaallll these years?

DOUG. I'm not hiding anything!

JOSH. All you DO is hide shit! You hide everything that means anything to you. Let's review! You hid being gay from your parents, you hid your break-up with Devon. Who knows what else? I can't take this shit anymore. I really can't. This is why Devon left without calling you. Yeah. Maybe he could never tell where you were at. And maybe your parents aren't upset that you're gay, they're just *hurt* you've been lying to them your whole life. Ever think about that?

DOUG. How can you say that to me?

JOSH. But that's the thing...

> *(***JOSH*** *stares off. He loses his thought.)*

Wait, what? I dunno what I's saying... Don' lissen t'me. I'm drunk. And I'm unhappy... I really am. I'm unhappy. Here's m'bottomline. Devon was a fucking idiot for treating you that way. And Jenna was a fucking idiot for what she did to me and Paige is a fucking idiot too. For fucking an idiot. They all messed up, and they made us...fight and feel stupid. 'Kay?

DOUG. Go to sleep.

JOSH. Yeah, I gotta go to sleep.

(He gets up with difficulty. Laughs.)

I am drunk!

(He walks toward his bedroom.)

Okay. Don't follow me, Joshy.

DOUG. I'm Doug. I won't. Goodnight.

JOSH. Yeah... I love you, Dougie. You know that right? Mmmm...

*(**JOSH** exits to his room.)*

DOUG. Jesus...

*(**DOUG** exhales slowly. He notices his hand shaking. He pulls it into his chest as tears well up in his eyes.)*

Transition

6. Living After Midnight

(November 5th, 2008 – 2:00 a.m.)

*(Obama's been president-elect for about three hours. **PAIGE** and **DOUG** come into a clean apartment. All of the **PAIGE** pictures are restored to the wall. **DOUG** has his headphones hanging around his neck. **PAIGE** and **DOUG** are exhausted and filled with joy.)*

PAIGE. This has been the best night ever. By far. Ever.

DOUG. You ain't lyin'.

PAIGE. What time is it now?

DOUG. Almost two.

PAIGE. Early! I'm so glad we cabbed it instead of waiting for the train. We'd still be waiting there. Let's have ice cream!

DOUG. It's kinda late for ice cream. My sensitive tummy!

PAIGE. Don't give me that. I bought us mint chocolate chip! *Breyer's.* The classiest of ice creams for this classy occasion.

DOUG. Alright.

PAIGE. Let's eat on the couch. And cuddle under the blankets!

DOUG. Well, we should probably be quiet since Josh is asleep...

PAIGE. Whatever, party pooper is asleep. I can't believe he left so early.

DOUG. You know he's got work tomorrow.

PAIGE. Like anyone at his job is gonna care if he's late or tired tomorrow considering tonight? The whole world is up partying and Josh is asleep. So typical.

DOUG. He was outside with us for an hour after the results came in.

PAIGE. You're always defending him.

DOUG. Because you're always attacking him. Stop being so negative!

PAIGE. You know what? You're right. You're totally right. It's gonna be a new day. A new administration. A new and lasting peace between Joshy and me.

DOUG. Thank God. Change we can believe in!

(He kicks off his shoes and then his pants to get more comfortable.)

Man, it's too cold in here. I need PJs.

(He goes in his room to get his pajama pants. **PAIGE** *gets the ice cream out of the freezer.)*

PAIGE. Hurry up! Do you think we'll ever see the city like that again? It's gotta be once in a lifetime.

DOUG. I don't know what could top it. You never know.

(He switches gears.)

I can't imagine Josh more excited. It's been nice to see something bring out his passion again. That kid needs a cause.

PAIGE. Yeah, I'm glad he got so involved this fall.

DOUG. It's like he's awake again.

PAIGE. Except for now when he's asleep.

(She giggles. Smiles to herself.)

DOUG. He looked really cute in his little election getup.

PAIGE. Yeah. I guess.

(She smiles thinking about him, as **DOUG** *knew she would.)*

DOUG. Do you have a crush on Josh?

PAIGE. Do YOU have a crush on Josh?

DOUG. He's worth a crush.

(He cranes his neck to make sure there's no activity from Josh's room.)

I'm just saying...if you wanted to with –

PAIGE. This from the guy who made me vow not to start anything when I moved in? What's going on with you tonight?

DOUG. With me? What about you? I think you spent more time watching Josh tonight than you did the results coming in.

PAIGE. Ha! Hardly!

DOUG. Matty's out of the picture, right?

PAIGE. I guess. Who knows?

DOUG. Maybe this is the time?

PAIGE. It's just...not.

DOUG. You guys are at each other's throats too much. You should just fuck already and get it out of your systems.

PAIGE. Doug!

DOUG. What?

PAIGE. You're gonna make me lose my appetite. What can restore me...?

(She closes her eyes and chants.)

ObamaObamaObama!

(She sighs in relief.)

There we go! Power of positive thinking.

DOUG. Fine. Deflect.

(**PAIGE** *finishes a spoonful before continuing.*)

PAIGE. It's not that there's *nothing* there, okay? It's just… never *right there*. You know? It's not ever right in front of me where it's like, "Yes! This now!" We just have bad timing. Something's always in the way.

DOUG. I just don't want the something in the way to be some promise you made to me.

PAIGE. It's not.

DOUG. 'Cause you actually promised "no weirdness" and we've had plenty of that.

PAIGE. Yeah, well, maybe if I'm really lucky? One day Josh and I will kiss, and then he'll immediately freak out and start telling me all the things he hates about me. That sounds really awesome. I'd like to see what that feels like.

DOUG. That's not what happened.

PAIGE. That's how you described it.

DOUG. Please don't bring this up again. He doesn't even remember it.

PAIGE. That's such bullshit. He does too.

DOUG. No, he was drunk off his ass that night. You didn't see how bad he got after you went to bed.

PAIGE. So?

DOUG. So, bringing it up now is only gonna make him feel bad.

PAIGE. He should apologize.

DOUG. Not necessary. It was stupid. And forever ago. Let's stay focused on tonight, please! And how awesome right now is!

PAIGE. Fine. Fine! Sorry I mentioned it. See? Apologies are easy.

DOUG. You're nuts.

(**DOUG** *eats a spoonful.*)

Mmm. This is my shit.

PAIGE. I know. It's so good.

(*They relax into each other.*)

It's neat having something new happen.

DOUG. It is.

PAIGE. I mean, I know almost everything will be the same, and the whole world is fucked up, but –

DOUG. It's nice to have hope.

PAIGE. What do you think his first big change is gonna be?

DOUG. I don't know. Gitmo, I guess.

PAIGE. Probably. And then Don't Ask-Don't Tell is gonna go away! Eee!

DOUG. You want I should join the army?

PAIGE. Well, no –

DOUG. Because I'm pretty sure the wars aren't going away.

PAIGE. What's wrong, D?

DOUG. Someone downtown said that Prop 8 passed.

PAIGE. What? No it didn't! They said it was too close to call. And there were progressive districts that still hadn't reported, so that should tip things.

DOUG. That's not what people were saying –

PAIGE. Well, who knows where the fuck they heard that. Let's just check the TV –

DOUG. Josh is sleeping –

PAIGE. Oh, who the fuck cares –

(**JOSH** *enters from his bedroom.*)

JOSH. Apparently, no one.

PAIGE. Joshy, I'm sorry I woke you up, but we wanted to check the TV about Prop 8 results, okay?

JOSH. They won't know for sure until tomorrow.

PAIGE. You're sure?

JOSH. Yeah, I checked just a little while ago. I need to pee. I'll be back.

(*He exits.*)

PAIGE. You see? It hasn't been decided.

DOUG. It's bad news that it's close.

PAIGE. You're not moving to LA anyway.

DOUG. Okay.

PAIGE. Listen, Obama's gonna repeal Don't Ask-Don't Tell, and then after that happens, everyone's gonna see how ridiculous banning gay marriage is and Congress will finally embrace it! Prop 8? Nullified.

DOUG. You've got it all planned out in your head.

PAIGE. You should too! You know what else I've got planned out?

DOUG. What...

PAIGE. Your gay wedding!

DOUG. Oh, GOD!

PAIGE. No, listen! It's gonna be so good.

DOUG. Who am I going to marry?

PAIGE. Oh that part doesn't matter!

DOUG. It doesn't?

PAIGE. Not when it comes to the ceremony!

(**JOSH** *re-enters wiping hands on shorts.*)

JOSH. What ceremony?

DOUG. Paige has lost her shit.

PAIGE. No, I haven't. Joshy come listen to my plan for Dougie's gay wedding in honor of Obama's win.

JOSH. Okay. I get to be Best Man.

PAIGE. No, I get to be Best Man. You can be an usher though.

JOSH. I wanna be Best Man!

PAIGE. Too bad. Doug asked me.

DOUG. No, I didn't!

PAIGE. Well, wouldn't you?

DOUG. No, I'd pick Josh.

JOSH. OH! That's gotta hurt.

PAIGE. Well who am I gonna be, Maid of Honor?

DOUG. That's up to the non-existent dude I'm supposed to marry.

PAIGE. What am I supposed to do at your wedding? Don't say sing. I wanna do more than sing.

DOUG. (*He thinks on it.*) You can officiate!

PAIGE. Officiate?

JOSH. Yeah, get one of those certificates online.

PAIGE. I'm not doing that! Then I have to wear some kinda bulky robe thing and I wanna look good!

JOSH. You don't have to dress like a priest.

DOUG. Yeah, you could still dress fabulous, and you'd be in the center of so many of the photos from the ceremony.

JOSH. It would be great.

PAIGE. Alright, *maybe*. But if I give in on Best Man, then you have to let me plan the rest of it because I have very specific ideas.

DOUG. Well, if you have all these great ideas, why don't you just save them for YOUR wedding?

PAIGE. Because I don't believe in marriage.

JOSH. What?

DOUG. So then why are you marrying me off?

PAIGE. Because I don't believe in marriage for me. I know you want to get married someday, and I definitely think you should have the right to if you want to, but I personally don't want to ever get married.

JOSH. Alrighty, I gotta go back to bed. You guys have fun with the future. Tomorrow's a new day!

DOUG. That it is. We did it.

JOSH. Yes! We! Did!

PAIGE. Hey, J! You didn't lose the camera on your way home, did you?

JOSH. No, it's in my coat. Right?

> *(He goes to his coat and finds a disposable camera.)*

Right! Oh, we've still got a shot left over.

DOUG. Group shot. Come on, Joshy! Get on the couch.

> *(**JOSH** smiles and falls into them on the couch. They rearrange themselves. **JOSH** holds the camera away from them and takes the photo. **PAIGE** stretches her legs over **JOSH**'s lap.)*

PAIGE. I hate disposables. I'm used to your digital. I wanna see how it turned out.

JOSH. I know. It sucks I forgot to charge the battery today. I'll bring it to Duane Reade tomorrow. You won't have to wait long.

PAIGE. Don't forget!

JOSH. I won't! Okay, Bedtime for Bonzo.

> (*He looks to* **PAIGE** *to move her legs.*)

PAIGE. Okay...

> (*She keeps them there.*)

JOSH. Can I get up?

PAIGE. Sure...

> (*She moves them and* **JOSH** *gets up. He walks to his bedroom door.*)

Hey. Come over here I want to tell you something.

> (**PAIGE** *jogs over, looks at* **JOSH**, *reconsiders what she's going to say, kisses his check and hugs him.*)

Thanks for staying out with us for a while after the results came in. I know you gotta work tomorrow.

JOSH. No problem! Sleep well, guys.

> (**JOSH** *exits to his bedroom.*)

PAIGE. See? Change you can believe in!

DOUG. Impressive. I'm going to bed too.

PAIGE. What? You said you'd stay up!

DOUG. I know. But I'm really tired. And now my tummy hurts.

PAIGE. You're mean.

DOUG. You're nuts.

PAIGE. LEH-LEH.

DOUG. I love you!

PAIGE. I love you too! You know, I never –

(*Paige's phone rings.*)

Who the F is calling me *now?* Huh, it's Matty.

DOUG. You gonna answer?

PAIGE. I guess.

(*She picks up.*)

Hey... Yeah, it's awesome! Yeah, we were downtown, Union Square... Oh, really? Well there were like a million people down there... Yeah, listen I gotta go. I need to talk to Doug before he goes to sleep. Yeah... we can do lunch, I guess...no, it depends on when I'm working...sure... Okay... Okay...you too. Goodnight.

(*She hangs up.*)

Ugh, now I have to go to lunch with him. I should've let it go to voicemail.

DOUG. The more things change...

PAIGE. Change is coming, D. It's gonna happen, and when it does I'm gonna have the biggest "I told you so!" waiting. *And* I'm gonna be Best Man.

DOUG. We'll see. Hopefully we won't be fifty when it happens.

PAIGE. By the time you hit thirty.

DOUG. That's some wishful thinking.

PAIGE. Gotta have hope.

DOUG. (*Mimicking how* **PAIGE** *does it.*) *Yeeeahh!*

(**PAIGE** *looks at him in gleeful surprise.*)

PAIGE. You did it!

DOUG. Just this one time and that's it!

PAIGE. We'll see! My influence is complete!

DOUG. You think so? "You love a heart forged in fire and brimstone."

PAIGE. ...Hey Dougie, you like him right?

DOUG. Obama? Yeah, I wanna have, like, a million of his babies.

PAIGE. No! Matty. *You* think he's a good guy.

DOUG. Yeah, I like him. Doesn't matter how I feel about him. Matters what *you* feel.

PAIGE. Yeah, I guess...

DOUG. Food for thought.

PAIGE. I'd rather have ice cream.

DOUG. Worry about it tomorrow then. G'night, Paige.

(*He exits to his room.* **PAIGE** *sits back on the couch with ice cream.*)

PAIGE. (*Sings.*) I got a crush on Obama...

Transition

7. Watch the Sunrise

(January 28, 2009 – 4:30 a.m.)

*(**JOSH** is sprawled out on the couch in the D.A.R.E. T-shirt and shorts. His Blackberry sits in the Berry Bowl that is now on the coffee table. It rings. He doesn't wake up. **PAIGE** opens the door and walks in carefully. She looks at where the table was. She turns and sees **JOSH** on the couch. She watches him for a moment. She walks over and sits on the arm of the couch. She opens her mouth to speak. She can't get herself to speak. She puts her hand on his leg. **JOSH** stirs. He blinks awake. He sees **PAIGE** there, but is confused. He thinks maybe he is dreaming.)*

PAIGE. Hey.

JOSH. Hey… You're here. Wait, what time is it?

(He looks at the clock.)

Jeez. What's going on? You alright?

*(**PAIGE** shakes her head.)*

About earlier, I'm sorry –

PAIGE. No.

JOSH. I am. I was a dick. I don't know what happened. I just… I didn't want to leave it like that.

PAIGE. I did. I left. I *left*. I'm sorry.

JOSH. You're here.

*(**PAIGE** leans in and kisses him. **JOSH** is initially shocked but reciprocates. They separate briefly and **PAIGE** puts her hands on his chest. She looks at his shirt and then back into his eyes.)*

PAIGE. You'd have to be wearing that shirt, wouldn't you?

JOSH. You want me to –?

> *(She nods. **JOSH** tries to take off his shirt, but it gets stuck just like it did with **DOUG**. **PAIGE** smiles and tries to help him. He gets it over his head, and a memory flickers.)*

Whoa, that's weird…

> *(**PAIGE** kisses him again. **PAIGE** takes her top off. **JOSH**'s shorts come off. He pauses.)*

You want to –

PAIGE. Fuck me.

> *(They get wrapped up in each other. **PAIGE** takes the lead in a way similar to **DOUG** from Game Night. **JOSH** pulls back. They look at each other and their momentum dies. **JOSH** is confused as memories fall back into place.)*

What's wrong?

JOSH. We did this before…

PAIGE. Uh, no. I'm really sure we didn't.

JOSH. I took off the…

> *(He thinks hard. It finally clicks.)*

It's Doug. "You took advantage of him." That's what you said earlier…

PAIGE. I did, but I –

JOSH. And then just now with the shirt, you –

> *(It all comes back.)*

Holy *shit.*

PAIGE. Josh –

JOSH. Nooo. I don't believe it! How fucked up am I?

PAIGE. You really didn't remember?

JOSH. No!

PAIGE. It's okay...

JOSH. What is okay? Nothing's okay. He told you?

PAIGE. Months later. We were drinking one night and it came out.

JOSH. We... I said horrible things to him. I *hurt* him. That's what you blame me for.

PAIGE. You should put your pants back on.

JOSH. Unbelievable. I wait how many fucking years for this moment and this is what happens.

PAIGE. Cock-blocked from the grave. That's impressive.

(*She can't help but laugh.*)

JOSH. This is funny?

(**PAIGE** *looks at him and laughs good-naturedly.* **JOSH** *starts to laugh despite himself.*)

You should never laugh at a guy when his pants are off. It really kills the mood.

PAIGE. Yeah well, you should never tell a girl kissing her reminds you of kissing your gay best friend. It really kills the mood.

JOSH. Yeah, no shit. Does Matty know you're here?

PAIGE. I told him I needed to stay at Amber's tonight. It's been a crazy day, to put it mildly.

JOSH. Do you feel badly about what happened just now?

PAIGE. No. Do you?

JOSH. A little.

PAIGE. We have a lot of shit to sort out. That was part of it. You okay?

JOSH. I'm okay…

PAIGE. He got over it. Whatever you said. He was good that way.

JOSH. I can never tell him I'm sorry. I *miss* him.

PAIGE. I know, babe. I know.

(She looks around the place.)

Does it feel to you like he's still here?

JOSH. Less and less. I mean, everything reminds me of him. But it's like the air is emptying. I wish I could hold on to it. Do you believe in ghosts?

PAIGE. Ghosts? No. I dunno… Why? Do *you* believe in ghosts?

JOSH. Not really. But…like years ago, after my mom died. Like a couple months after it, I was in our house, alone and I was in my room, doing whatever. Just sitting around. And this wave came over me, and I got goosebumps, and I just knew my mom was downstairs. I knew it. There was this energy and I knew exactly where it was and who it was…but I didn't know why it was there. And I was so freaked out. I couldn't face it. I just ran out of my house. Just right out the front door and I didn't look back. I ran for two blocks over to my friend Jessie's house. Her mom let me in, and I told them what happened, and they just sat with me until the feeling went away. It was so random, it wasn't a special day, there was nothing going on…but I so truly *felt* it.

PAIGE. Jeez…

JOSH. I don't know if this'll make sense… I knew that Doug's parents were gonna come and they were gonna take all his stuff, all his real stuff and I guess…part of me wanted something here as like an anchor for him. That's why I kept the chair. In case he exists out there somewhere and sometime in the middle of the night – or the middle of a day – if he needs to, he could connect to something that was still here and he'd…have some place to sit. And if I got that feeling that he was here, I wouldn't run away this time. It's stupid…

> (**JOSH** *is shaken and embarrassed.* **PAIGE** *goes over to him and puts her hand on his shoulder.*)

PAIGE. No, it's not. Okay, it's a little weird. But it's nice.

> (*They sit silently for a moment.*)

Inauguration sucked. You watched, right? You must've.

JOSH. Yeah, sure. At work.

PAIGE. I watched at Matty's. He was in DC so it was… quiet. I wound up turning it off after like five minutes. It was this beautiful historic moment for everyone else, and I was just *seething* inside that Doug wasn't there. It was all I could feel. It's pretty much all I can still feel. This…

> (*There are no words. She just shakes her clenched fists in front of her.*)

There was so much he was looking forward to. It's not fair. I've been thinking a lot about…thinking. I mean, my brain goes at like a hundred miles a minute, right? And yours must go double mine. Nerd. But there are all these things up there that I constantly think about. He had to be thinking about stuff, right before he died. It makes me really sad to think about that. I wonder if it's different if you're old. Or if you're really sick, or something? I wonder if something clicks in your brain then and you stop thinking forward. If you just stop making plans. I don't want to be planning anything when I die. I don't want to be cheated out of realizing a good idea.

JOSH. All I can think is… Doug's never gonna be thirty. It was like this thing that was coming, and he was excited for it, and now it's never gonna get there. He had so much inside him…and I think if it had been me instead… I don't know. I think Jenna was right. I'm not working toward anything. I look back on my twenties it's like I didn't do anything –

PAIGE. Okay, that's not true. We did work that mattered. It mattered to you and it mattered to all those kids. You're gonna find the next thing that inspires you.

JOSH. I'm scared that what happened to Doug's gonna happen to me.

PAIGE. Well, it's a scary thought.

JOSH. How are we gonna get past it?

PAIGE. …I'm gonna go with you to Doug's parents.

JOSH. You sure?

PAIGE. It's the right thing to do. Plus, it's the best chance I'll get to steal back his Discman.

JOSH. Heh. Yeah…

PAIGE. I'm sorry for what I said this afternoon. I took it too far.

JOSH. Was he in love with me, Paige? Do you think?

PAIGE. He loved you. That's for damn sure. Sometimes… I think we can love people without being in love with them, but we love them so much we run out of normal ways to show them…and then we do stupid things.

JOSH. Yeah.

(**PAIGE** *yawns.*)

PAIGE. It's late... I'm gonna turn in, I guess.

(She gets up and walks toward her bedroom.)

JOSH. Now?

PAIGE. Yeah. Before the sun rises. You go to sleep too.

JOSH. We could...not sleep alone tonight.

(She takes a breath.)

PAIGE. Tonight, I need one last night alone in my room. And you should spend one last night in yours. And tomorrow, I will talk to Matty. That oughta be fun. And tomorrow, you will look into finding a new apartment. Which should also be fun. And then tomorrow night...

JOSH. Yeah?

PAIGE. Tomorrow. Goodnight, Joshy.

JOSH. Goodnight, Paige.

(She exits to her room. **JOSH** *exits to his room.)*

Transition

8. I Hope Tomorrow is Like Today

(The following scene flows like a dream-like version of the first scene. The kitchen table is back. It's morning. **DOUG** *is on the couch.* **PAIGE** *walks in.)*

DOUG. Good morning!

PAIGE. *(Sing-song.)* No, it's not. 'Cause I'm awake!

DOUG. Sleep okay?

PAIGE. Not really. I feel like I had crazy dreams, but I can't remember them now. You know when you have that?

DOUG. Uh huh. It's the worst.

(**PAIGE** *starts to feels strange. Déjà vu is kicking in.)*

PAIGE. Josh up yet?

DOUG. Just got out of the shower. Bathroom's –

(He notices her confusion.)

What's up?

PAIGE. Déjà vu. I feel like we've done this before.

DOUG. We do this every morning.

PAIGE. Yeah, I guess so. It's such a creepy feeling.

DOUG. Yeah. Bathroom's all yours.

PAIGE. I can't believe how late I slept. I'm supposed to be leaving now. I just can't wake up…

DOUG. There's coffee, if you want coffee.

PAIGE. I wish. My throat's still killing me.

DOUG. Still?

PAIGE. STILL. It's really bad this morning.

DOUG. Test results come back…?

PAIGE. Tomorrow, supposedly.

DOUG. Paige, I really think it's mono.

PAIGE. Ugh, it can't be mono. That shit will never go away.

DOUG. Sorry, babe. You've had this thing too long.

PAIGE. Dougie, you're supposed to tell me it's not serious and it's gonna go away.

DOUG. *(With no conviction.)* It's not serious and it's gonna go away.

PAIGE. Thanks.

(Goes to look out the window.)

Is it supposed to effing snow today?

DOUG. NY1 just said partly cloudy. No snow.

PAIGE. They are such LIARS. Look out a FUCKING WINDOW NY1.

DOUG. It's gonna be cold. Dress warm.

PAIGE. This sucks.

(She scratches at her throat.)

How are *you*, Dougie?

> *(***PAIGE*** goes directly to get the apple cider vinegar in the cabinet.)*

DOUG. I'm alright.

> *(***PAIGE*** gets ready to gargle.)*

My head really hurts.

PAIGE. Uh huh.

DOUG. I fell on the stairs coming down Morningside Park last night. There was ice and I didn't see it and I totally wiped out a couple steps before the landing. I got lucky though. Just a little banged up.

(**PAIGE** *gargles. Spits into the sink.*)

PAIGE. Wait, what did you say?

DOUG. I fell down the stairs in the park last night. You listen to nothing.

PAIGE. Are you okay?

DOUG. Yeah, just a little scraped up, but my head is pounding this morning.

PAIGE. You should get it checked out.

DOUG. It's fine.

PAIGE. No, come with me to the hospital today when I go to First Thought.

DOUG. Yeah so they can charge me three hundred bucks just to walk in the door? It's a headache.

PAIGE. No, just come in with me and someone will check you out on the side, unofficially. Oh, wait.

DOUG. What?

PAIGE. I'm not going to the hospital today. I have to teach a workshop in the Bronx in, like, forty-five minutes. I should already be out the door.

DOUG. Call in sick so you can rest.

PAIGE. I called in sick last week. First Thought doesn't give paid sick days. If you'd like me to have my share of the rent this month, then I'm gonna have to go to work at some point.

DOUG. C'mon, Josh will cover you if you're short.

(*She gives him a look.*)

Since you're sick! He spotted me last month. He'll do it for you.

> (**JOSH** *enters, he's dressed in business clothes for work.*)

JOSH. What will he do for you?

PAIGE. Look good in a fitted dress shirt. That's what he'll do. Oww!

> (*She grabs her throat from sharp pain.*)

Oww...

JOSH. How you feeling?

PAIGE. Like shit, how 'bout you?

JOSH. Hmmm...better than that, thankfully.

DOUG. She finds out if it's mono tomorrow.

PAIGE. It's *not.*

JOSH. I kinda want...

> (*Something stirs in him. This situation is not right.*)

PAIGE. What?

JOSH. Never mind. Have you guys seen my Blackberry lying around?

DOUG. NO. This is why I got you that dish for Christmas so you could put it there and not lose it. Why are you not using the Berry Bowl?

JOSH. I know, I know.

DOUG. I decorated it and everything.

JOSH. I love the Berry Bowl. The Berry Bowl is awesome. I just always put it down weird places without realizing. Is it in the couch?

(**JOSH** *slides over the back of the couch on top of* **DOUG**, *as he does in Scene 1. Being close to* **DOUG** *makes* **JOSH** *very happy.)*

DOUG. Get off!

(**DOUG** *dumps* **JOSH** *off onto the floor. He takes this opportunity to look under the couch and coffee table. No dice.)*

It's not here.

JOSH. Fuuuuck. I don't have time to go on a big search for it.

(**JOSH** *tries to exit to his room.)*

PAIGE. Oh, I saw it…

JOSH. Oh, where?

PAIGE. Someplace weird… Look in the kitchen.

JOSH. Okay…

(*He heads into the kitchen.* **PAIGE** *walks over to* **DOUG** *on the couch and looks at the TV screen.)*

PAIGE. You and Pat Kiernan.

DOUG. He's cute!

PAIGE. What time are you going into work?

(*She goes back into the kitchen.)*

DOUG. Noon.

PAIGE. Then why the hell are you up?

DOUG. Can't sleep. I have a headache. I'm waiting to take some more Motrin before I go back to bed.

PAIGE. Joshy, Doug hurt his head and he won't get it checked out.

JOSH. Get it checked out, Doug.

DOUG. I'm fine, Josh.

JOSH. He's fine, Paige.

PAIGE. Ugh, alright. I don't have the energy.

DOUG. *(To **JOSH**.)* Any luck?

JOSH. No. Can you –

DOUG. On it.

> *(He reaches for his phone.)*

JOSH. Oh wait.

> *(He opens the drawer.)*

Yes! Got it.

DOUG. Where?

JOSH. Utensil drawer. Thanks, D. Ugh, I'm gonna be late.

> *(He exits to his room.)*

DOUG. Any good e-mails?

PAIGE. Hmm? No... I was hoping to get a message about a callback, but there's nothing.

DOUG. Sorry.

PAIGE. Whatever, no big loss.

> *(**JOSH** rushes back in and points to laptop.)*

JOSH. Okay, I'm gonna need that back. I can't be late today.

DOUG. Scarf?

JOSH. Scarf...

> *(He spins back around and exits into his room again. **DOUG** and **PAIGE** share a snarky look.)*

DOUG. I want cereal.

> *(He moves toward the kitchen to gather supplies. **PAIGE** watches his warily.)*

Hey, are you gonna take a shower? That'll make you feel a little better.

PAIGE. I don't have the time or energy to shower. They can smell me today.

DOUG. What's your plan post-work?

PAIGE. Let's see: I'm teaching this morning, meeting Matty for a late lunch, picking up dry cleaning, and then coming home to sleep FOREVER.

DOUG. If you do too much, it makes it worse.

PAIGE. I know. Thank you, Doctor Doug.

DOUG. And take Tylenol every four hours to keep your fever down.

PAIGE. I will, Doctor.

DOUG. I had mono, jerk. I'm trying to help you.

PAIGE. I know. I appreciate it.

> *(**JOSH** re-enters.)*

JOSH. Okay, scarf. Blackberry. iPod. Laptop. I am good to go.

PAIGE. Keys?

JOSH. Keys!

DOUG. Bathroom.

DOUG & JOSH. Soap dish.

JOSH. Jinx. Yeaaah!

> *(He runs to get them.)*

Okay, I'm out of here.

DOUG. We hanging out tonight?

JOSH. I think so. I'll call you later. You feel better, okay?

DOUG. Josh! Charger!

JOSH. Always with this thing! I'm so fucking careless.

DOUG. More like willfully ignorant.

JOSH. I know. I'm lame. Forgive me?

DOUG. I do.

JOSH. Good!

> *(He makes a biting motion toward **DOUG**'s cheek. **DOUG** smiles. **JOSH** takes the charger.)*

Thanks for this! Bye!

> *(**JOSH** exits. **PAIGE** watches the door and then **DOUG**. They sit in silence for a moment as **DOUG** eats.)*

PAIGE. Doug? Wanna do me a favor?

DOUG. No. What is it?

PAIGE. Don't die.

> *(He continues to eat. He repeats himself as if she had not spoken.)*

DOUG. What is it?

PAIGE. You wanna go teach a bunch of really great, *really* attentive high school kids about methods of contraception for me so I can stay here and sleep?

DOUG. Not so much.

PAIGE. Curse you.

DOUG. I am cursed.

> (**PAIGE** *pretends to zap* **DOUG** *with her hands and makes a "spell-casting noise" then promptly starts hack coughing.*)

DOUG. Just calm down. See what happens when you act evil?

PAIGE. How long is this gonna last, D?

DOUG. If it's mono, it can stay with you for a long time. It was really six months or so before all the symptoms went away for me.

PAIGE. Matty is gonna break up with me.

DOUG. You guys break up all the time.

PAIGE. Well this time for good. I'm gonna be a bad girlfriend who has no energy to do anything and just wants to complain all the time.

DOUG. You can always complain to me.

PAIGE. You promise?

DOUG. Promise. You can complain to me and fight with Josh and give all your nice time to Matty.

PAIGE. He doesn't deserve all of it.

> (*She slumps.*)

DOUG. (*He taps his neck.*) Energy!

PAIGE. (*She taps her neck halfheartedly.*) Energy! Okay, coat…

DOUG. Maybe you should put on real pants?

PAIGE. Yeah, that would help.

> (**PAIGE** *goes to her room.* **DOUG** *gets up and puts Paige's gloves in her coat pockets. Sits back down to eat.*)

Do you have anything lined up this week?

DOUG. Chorus calls Thursday and Friday. It's a national tour on Friday. It'd be awesome if I got that.

PAIGE. If you're on tour, how am I gonna complain to you? You're already breaking promises!

DOUG. You can call. Text.

(**PAIGE** *re-enters in better casual clothing.*)

PAIGE. Texting. The height of human comfort.

DOUG. It's too bad you can't come out with us tonight.

(**PAIGE** *gets up to get her coat.*)

PAIGE. Boys' night out. If you come home and I'm sprawled out on the floor, please just step over me.

DOUG. We'll roll you out of the way of foot traffic. Don't worry.

PAIGE. Thanks! Okay I'm off.

DOUG. You're my hero, Paige!

PAIGE. Awesome. That will carry me through. I'm not kissing you, cuz I'm sick.

DOUG. I'm not scared. Gimme love.

PAIGE. Okay.

(*They kiss on the cheek and* **DOUG** *looks at her for real recognition of the moment, but she's back on track.*)

Bye, babe! Talk to you later.

DOUG. Love you!

PAIGE. I love you too.

(*She exits the apartment.*)

DOUG. Okay then.

(**DOUG** *keeps eating. He rubs his head, swallows and sits still. He gets up with his bowl, moves his chair back to where it is tucked away in the kitchen. Light fades on the dining area.* **DOUG** *puts his bowl in the sink and walks back to the couch. Light goes out on the kitchen area.* **DOUG** *walks back into the bathroom and closes the door. Sunlight comes in through the window.* **PAIGE** *re-enters wearing the clothes she wore in Scene 7. She is having a hard time remembering what is real and what is not.* **JOSH** *enters from his room looking much the same. They see each other as the weight of the world settles in. They are not happy. They are not sad. They are coping.*)

JOSH. Morning.

PAIGE. Morning.

End of Play